# There's One in Every Family

# There's One in Every Family

Candice F. Ransom

AN
**APPLE**
PAPERBACK

SCHOLASTIC INC.
New York Toronto London Auckland Sydney

ISBN 0-590-42977-9



12 11 10 9 8 7 6 5 4 3 2 1 2 3 4 5/9

Printed in the U.S.A. 40

First Scholastic printing, December 1990

# 1

It was a slow news day on Wagner Avenue.

Millicent Adams let go of the tree branch long enough to push her pencil behind her ears. Like a real newspaper reporter, she thought. Unfortunately, the pencil became tangled in her hair and she had to pull it out again, with a painful grimace. Millicent's hair was medium brown, medium length, and usually untidy.

She thought she might see something exciting if she climbed a tree. Even high up in the pear tree in Roberta's yard, Millicent could see nothing was happening.

Two branches below her, Roberta Holloway said, "Can we get down now? All we've seen in the past hour is Mr. Vandor walking his dog. That's hardly news."

"Let's wait a few more minutes," Millicent said optimistically. "Something might happen. Good reporters are patient. That's how they get their stories."

Roberta leaned against the trunk and unzipped her jacket. It was very warm for the last week in

December. She fiddled with the paper lift ticket fastened to the zipper. Roberta had spent four days of the Christmas vacation in Colorado, on a ski trip with her parents. The ticket allowed Roberta to ride the ski lift up the mountain as often as she wanted. Millicent thought Roberta ought to take the ticket off her jacket now that she was back in Virginia where there were no ski lifts for miles and miles.

"This is a dumb day," Roberta declared. "My father says the week between Christmas and New Year's is the dullest week in the year."

Millicent felt her friend had no right to complain. At least Roberta had been to Colorado. Millicent hadn't been anywhere, except this pear tree in Roberta's front yard. She agreed with her friend, though. It *was* turning out to be a dumb day.

"The calendar people ought to mark dumb days on the calendar," she said. "Like holidays, so we'd know when the next one is coming."

"And I could plan to be in Colorado," Roberta said. "Or Disney World." Last Christmas vacation, Roberta's parents took her to Florida. "Did I ever tell you about the Haunted Mansion? It was so neat — "

"Keep watching. You might let a story slip by." Millicent didn't want to hear about Roberta's trips to far-flung places. They were supposed to be working on that day's issue of the *Wagner Avenue*

*Chronicle.* "We have our subscribers to think about," she added virtuously.

"Three subscribers," Roberta said, with disgust. "My parents, your parents, and Mrs. Taylor. We only make thirty cents on our newspaper. You said we'd make a dollar every day."

Millicent shifted to find a more comfortable position on her branch. Tree-sitting was boring. "I thought everybody on our street would sign up. Can I help it if people don't want to support local enterprises?" This last phrase was borrowed from her mother, who ran a neighborhood food co-op. Mrs. Adams bought large quantities of produce from local farmers, usually green things like kale and Brussels sprouts.

"There are ten houses on our street," Millicent went on. "I thought all ten would buy a copy of our newspaper. Where else can they read news about their very own street?"

"There are ten houses but only *nine* families," Roberta corrected. "You forgot the house on the corner is empty."

"So I made one little mistake. The *idea* is still good. If we had a really juicy story, everybody would buy a copy in a flash," Millicent said. "Probably even the people in Maple Hills would buy a copy."

Maple Hills was the big housing development on the other side of Wagner Avenue. For some reason their little street was never finished. It dead-ended at a concrete barricade. A short field stretched beyond the barricade, dividing the subdivision from Wagner Avenue.

"*If* we had a juicy story," Roberta mentioned. "That's a pretty big if, especially on a day as dumb as this one."

Millicent had dreamed up the idea of a neighborhood newspaper the last day of school before Christmas vacation. She figured she and Roberta could print up a single-page newspaper and sell each copy for a dime. They'd be guaranteed a dollar a day, ten cents for each of the ten houses, which they'd split. Well, ninety cents, anyway, if everyone subscribed. It wouldn't cost them a thing except paper. Millicent would borrow her father's typewriter. Roberta's father had a copy machine he'd let them use. And the news was free.

But hard to come by, she was finding out.

They had lots of stories for the first issue of the newspaper. "Turkey Dinner a Big Success," "Boy Falls into Christmas Tree" (Millicent's little brother Rudy, who was trying to put the star on top), and "Nine-Year-Old Girl Youngest Newspaper Mogul." This last item was about Millicent herself. Since it was mostly her newspaper, she figured she could toot her own horn.

When her older sister Abby read this, she'd hooted with laughter. "You don't even know what 'mogul' means."

"Yes, I do," Millicent had replied. She collected interesting words. It was her hobby. "A mogul is somebody who runs a newspaper and lives in a castle."

This cracked up Abby even more. "She means William Randolph Hearst!" she reported gleefully to their father. "Millicent, Hearst wasn't the only mogul in business."

"I know. Now there's me. So that makes two of us."

Roberta didn't like Millicent hogging the headlines, and insisted on a feature about *her* in the next day's paper. "Fourth-Grader Skis down Bunny Slope" told about Roberta's adventures in Colorado.

Millicent thought her own story was better. It was a lot more important to be a newspaper mogul than to slide down a snow-covered hill with sticks strapped to your feet.

Although Millicent and Roberta shared writing the stories, Millicent made up the daily horoscope ("Libra — this is your lucky day!"), figured out the *next day's* weather, for who'd want to read about today's weather when they could just look out the window, and even drew a comic strip. She was especially proud of the masthead she designed. The masthead was the part of the paper with the title and the date and price of the paper.

*The Wagner Avenue Chronicle*
The Only Newspaper About Life on
Wagner Avenue, in
Fairfax, Virginia, in

The United States of America, in
The Western Hemisphere, in
The World, in
The Solar System, in
The Milky Way Galaxy, in
The Universe
Millicent T. Adams, Editor-in-Chief

The heading was very large. In fact, it took up half the page, but Millicent thought the extra information gave her paper a professional look. Besides, a lot of people didn't know what galaxy they lived in.

Naturally Roberta demanded equal billing on the masthead. Millicent argued that there could only be one editor-in-chief and that was her. But to keep peace she added, underneath her name and title, *Roberta Holloway, Ace Reporter.*

Right now, though, neither of them were ace reporters. They didn't have one single story for that day's issue.

Yesterday had been just as bad. The big news story was about Mr. Adams' bald spot.

" 'Forty-Nine-Year-Old Man Loses Hair,' " Mr. Adams read out loud unbelievingly when Millicent handed him his copy of the paper. "Millicent, is nothing sacred in this house?"

Millicent had been desperate for news and the little hairless circle on the back of her father's head, which he'd just discovered, was the only newsworthy story that came to mind. Today they didn't even have a bald spot to write about.

"My foot's gone to sleep," Roberta said. "I'm getting down." She began shinnying down the trunk.

With a sigh, Millicent tucked her notebook and pencil in her pocket. She climbed down the tree, jumping on the wet ground with a spongy thud. It had rained during the holidays, but hadn't snowed so far. "My father says it's too warm to snow," Roberta said. She had a comment for everything. "If you want snow, go to Colorado."

"You know," Millicent said thoughtfully, "it's winter now. People aren't going to be doing much outside. The big news stories are happening *in*-doors. We need to go from house to house and ask people if they have any news. I bet we get a story at every stop." She'd leave her own house until last — her father wasn't happy about making yesterday's headlines.

"OK," Roberta agreed. "Want to start with the Sanders?"

Millicent wrinkled her nose. "Might as well. Get it over with."

The Sanders family lived next door to Millicent. The parents were OK, but the two kids gave Millicent a pain. Craig Sanders was in Rudy's second-grade class at school. He was a little bully, always picking on Rudy. Millicent couldn't understand why her little brother played with Craig and even called him his best friend. Sheila was Craig's sister. She whined over every little thing and never shared her toys. Millicent was glad Sheila was a third-grader and not in fourth grade with her and Roberta.

They walked up to the Sanders' porch. Millicent rapped businesslike on the door, hoping Mrs. Sanders would answer.

The door swung open, but instead of Mrs. Sanders, Sheila stood there. "We don't want any," she said rudely and started to close the door.

Millicent stuck her foot out, preventing Sheila from closing the door. "Is your mother home?" she asked in a withering tone. It was the only way to deal with kids like Sheila.

"No. She's out. What do you want with her?"

"We want to know if she has any news for our paper," Roberta answered, narrowing her green eyes at Sheila. "We have some extra space in today's issue." An understatement, but the truth.

"Are you guys still messing with that stupid newspaper?" Sheila scoffed. "Nobody reads it."

"A lot you know," Millicent said in her haughtiest newspaper-mogul voice. "We might even win a Poolitzer Prize this year. That's the prize they give to the best newspapers."

"Well, yours won't win." Sheila moved an enormous wad of bubble gum to her left cheek.

"Do you have any news or not?" Millicent was getting impatient. "We have a deadline to meet."

Sheila snapped her gum. "OK. Here's our news. My stupid brother got in trouble this morning and he has to stay in his room all afternoon. My mother is out shopping. She's buying me a new dress to wear to Stephanie Watson's birthday party. My dad came home early from work. That's it." She shoved the door shut. Millicent barely got her foot out in time.

"I can't stand that kid," she remarked, as they headed down the sidewalk.

"You know why Sheila acts like that?" Roberta said.

"Because she's a brat, that's why."

"No, it's because she's the favorite kid. Her parents like her the best. Better than Craig."

"Well, who can blame them? Craig is such a bully. He broke Rudy's truck yesterday, the one he just got for Christmas. I know he did it on purpose. And then he hit Rudy and made him cry." Then Millicent asked, "How do you know Sheila's the favorite?"

"You can just tell," Roberta said. "Her mom is always buying her things at the store. And Sheila never gets in trouble and she's as bad as her brother. There's a favorite in every family."

Millicent digested this. Usually Roberta was right about such things. What was it like to be the family favorite? she wondered. To be the favored one, the one everybody liked best? If there was a favorite in every family, as Roberta claimed, then who was the favorite in Millicent's family? She wasn't sure.

Roberta pushed her shiny black bangs out of her eyes. "I'm glad I'm an only child. I know who the favorite kid is in my family. Me!"

Besides being an only child, an enviable position, Millicent always thought, Roberta was adopted. Millicent sometimes wished she was an adopted child, so she could have a million toys and go to neat places like Colorado and Disney World.

But being the favorite child was just as good. Maybe even better. In Roberta's house, her parents *had* to make Roberta their favorite. There wasn't anyone else to choose from. In a family of four kids, like Millicent's, it would be a great honor to be the favorite, the one everyone liked best.

"I don't know if we have a favorite kid in our family," Millicent said. She'd never thought about it before.

"There has to be."

"If we have one, I'm the favorite in my house," Millicent declared boldly.

Roberta looked at her sharply, as if she suspected Millicent was fibbing. "Are you sure it isn't Rudy? The youngest is usually the favorite."

"No, it's me."

"Are you your mother's favorite or your father's favorite?" Roberta asked.

Millicent didn't realize that favorite kids were put in separate categories. "Everybody's favorite. Both my parents like me better than Rudy or Abby or Geneva. So does my grandmother Helena in Michigan. And my aunt Pat. They like me the best of any of us kids." They probably *did* if they ever thought about it.

Roberta still wore a doubtful expression.

"Well, I *am*," Millicent persisted. "I'll prove it. Come with me to my house. I'll ask my mother who the favorite child is. She'll tell you."

She knew she was taking an awful chance. What if her mother announced that Geneva was her favorite child? It was possible. Geneva was the oldest. She didn't live at home any more. She was married to Lyman Renquist and was expecting a baby in February. Mrs. Adams talked about Geneva and the coming baby all the time.

Her mother was in the laundry room. Mrs. Adams claimed she washed more clothes than anyone in Fairfax County.

"Mom?" Millicent called hesitantly. "I have to ask you something. Something real important." She was keenly aware of Roberta right beside her, waiting for the answer.

"What is it?" her mother said, stuffing clothes into the washer.

"Who is the favorite child in our family? Out of me and Rudy and Abby and Geneva. Who do you like best?"

"Now you know there are no favorites in our family, Millicent. Your father and I like all of our children equally."

Millicent was disappointed. "Roberta says every family has a favorite. It's a proven fact," she said emphatically. "Think about it, Mom. You must like *one* of us a little bit better than the others."

"I don't," she said lightly. "I love you all the same."

"*Exactly* the same?"

"Exactly."

Millicent turned to Roberta. "So much for your theory. This family doesn't have any favorites."

"It's not you, either," Roberta was quick to point out as they left the laundry room.

"Well, if my family ever picked a favorite, I'd be it." She felt safe saying this now. Her mother hadn't put her on the spot and declared Rudy or Abby to be the favorite.

They went through the kitchen. Papers were spread all over the kitchen table. Mrs. Adams was president of the PTA at Millicent's school that year. She was also head of a committee to build a new playground for Green Acres Elementary. The playground committee kept her mother busy.

"Hey, this could be our story for today's paper," Roberta said. " 'Family with Four Children Has No Favorites.' I bet your family is the only one on our street with no favorite kids."

Snatching a couple of apples from the bowl on the counter, the girls went back outside to sit on the steps in the thin winter sunshine. At last they had their news story for the day. And since Millicent had already written the horoscope ("Gemini — look under your bed for a surprise.") and tomorrow's weather forecast ("Still no snow in sight."), they could relax a moment before tackling the typewriter.

"I wonder how a person gets to be the favorite?" Millicent said, biting into her apple.

Roberta tossed her apple core into the garbage can by the back steps. "Easy. Be helpful. Like Stacey Morrison."

Stacey Morrison was the teacher's pet in their class at school. She was forever carrying Mrs. Stann's books and erasing the blackboard. Her method must work because Mrs. Stann almost always chose Stacey to deliver the lunch money to the office.

"Sheila Sanders isn't helpful and she's the favorite in *her* family," Millicent contradicted.

Roberta shrugged. "Sheila's a fluke. Her parents probably like her the best because she's not as awful as her brother." She stood. "I have to go home now. Bring the paper over when it's finished and we'll make copies on my father's machine."

Millicent had forgotten about the newspaper. She was thinking. If her parents had never chosen a favorite child in their family, then the position was open, wasn't it? Waiting for somebody to fill it. Why not her? *She'd* become the favorite person in her family.

And she'd do it by being helpful, so nobody could say it was a fluke that Millicent T. Adams was the favorite Adams child.

After all, she was already a newspaper mogul and an editor-in-chief. Becoming the family favorite shouldn't be too much of a challenge.

# 2

When that day's issue of the *Wagner Avenue Chronicle* was finished, Millicent made four copies on Mr. Holloway's copy machine. One for Roberta's family, one for Millicent's family, one for Mrs. Taylor, and an extra they hoped to sell. If they had four subscribers instead of three, then the profits would be easier to split. Twenty cents a day seemed like a lot more money than fifteen cents a day. Millicent wondered if that other newspaper mogul, William Randolph Hearst, started out this way, with only three subscribers.

Roberta had to stay inside, so Millicent took Rudy with her to deliver Mrs. Taylor's paper. She also took Jocko, her stuffed monkey. Her grandmother Helena had made Jocko when Millicent was two years old. He was more than a toy — he was her oldest friend. Jocko had been stitched from grayish-brown hunting socks. The red and white heel of the sock formed his smiling face. Millicent's grandmother had sewed on flat black buttons for his eyes and a jaunty cap topped with a red pom-pom.

When Millicent was little, Jocko went wherever she went. Now Jocko usually stayed on Millicent's bed, where she could talk to him when she needed a pair of ears to listen to her troubles. Jocko never told her he was too busy, or had to go inside and do his homework — he was always there.

Today Millicent decided her monkey needed a little outing. Rudy came, too, because he liked to be with Millicent. Unlike most girls she knew who had little brothers, Millicent enjoyed having Rudy around. He looked up to her and that made her feel good. She remembered a long time ago, when she rode the minibus to kindergarten. Mrs. Adams had waited on the corner with Millicent, holding Rudy's hand. Rudy was only three years old, but he had to have a red plastic lunchbox just like Millicent's. When the bus came, he waved good-bye as if he'd never see her again. Having a brother like Rudy made Millicent feel good.

Early winter twilight fell around them like a lavender mist as they scaled the steep hill above the Adams' house.

Alma Taylor lived on top of the hill. She was an old lady who raised African violets and Persian cats. The neighborhood kids once thought Mrs. Taylor was the grouchiest woman in the state, but Millicent had become friendly with Mrs. Taylor last fall. She learned an astonishing secret — that her neighbor had once been a Hollywood fashion designer.

Mrs. Taylor's house was the biggest on Wagner

Avenue. It was made of wood, not brick, and had a big porch across the front. The house was painted a welcoming yellow, with dark green trim.

It took Mrs. Taylor several minutes to answer the door. She had arthritis and walked with the aid of a cane.

"Millicent! And Rudy!" she cried happily. "Come in, my dears. I see you brought Jocko. I've just made scones. You can help me eat them."

Millicent exchanged a grin with Rudy. She had been hoping Mrs. Taylor had baked something good. Sometimes when Millicent and Roberta visited, Mrs. Taylor would fix a tea tray from which she served in the living room, as if she and Roberta were grown-ups.

They followed Mrs. Taylor down the hall. Three Persian cats escorted them, and at least five more lounged on the plush chairs and sofas in the living room.

Rudy got down on the floor to play with a black kitten named Allison. Mrs. Taylor gave all her cats people names. No Snowball or Fluffy for her.

"I'll just be a minute." Mrs. Taylor thumped into the kitchen.

"That's Mrs. Taylor at Loretta Young's wedding," Millicent said, indicating a silver-framed photograph on the mantle. "Loretta Young was a famous Hollywood actress."

Rudy wasn't much interested. "This cat's chewing my hair!"

It seemed hard to believe that someone as important as Alma Taylor lived on their little street. Mrs. Taylor preferred to keep her past a secret, though. "I put up with enough hoopla back in Hollywood," she told Millicent once. "Now I just want peace and quiet."

"Millicent," Mrs. Taylor called from the kitchen. "Would you do the honors, my dear?"

Millicent carried the heavy silver tea tray into the living room and set it carefully on the coffee table. Mrs. Taylor settled herself in her green velvet high-backed chair that reminded Millicent of a throne and poured a few drops of tea into delicate china cups, adding generous amounts of milk and sugar. She gave a cup each to Millicent and Rudy before pouring a stronger cup for herself.

"It's Earl Grey," Millicent said knowledgeably to her brother. "The best tea in the world." She didn't tell Rudy that she once thought Earl Grey was one of the cats.

"And this is for Jocko." Mrs. Taylor handed Millicent a tiny doll's cup filled with milk. "We can't leave him out now, can we?" Mrs. Taylor was the only grown-up, outside of family, who understood Jocko's significance.

Millicent solemnly set the tiny cup in front of her monkey. "Don't spill it," she admonished. "You either," she warned Rudy. Her brother had never been to one of Mrs. Taylor's tea parties before. Millicent worried about him breaking and spilling things.

"Have a scone," Mrs. Taylor offered politely. Millicent refrained from grabbing two or three of the sweet biscuits. At home, she had to snatch fast or wind up with crumbs, but here she remembered her manners.

"I'm so glad you brought the paper," Mrs. Taylor said, handing Millicent two nickels. "I look forward to reading it every evening. Such interesting goings-on right in our neighborhood." She picked up the single sheet and glanced at the headline. "No favorites in the Adams family, eh? A democratic family. Everyone treated the same."

Millicent was anxious to talk about family favorites. Rudy had gulped his tea and was back down on the floor with the black kitten. He wasn't really listening to the conversation.

"Who was the favorite person in your family?" she asked. Mrs. Taylor could be counted on for an honest response. She wouldn't put Millicent off with an "I don't know" or "nobody."

Mrs. Taylor set her cup down with a delicate clink. "Well, according to my brother, I was, because I was the youngest and a girl. But I believed he was, because he was the oldest and a boy. It all depended on where you stood, you see."

"But who do you think was the favorite?" Millicent pressed. "Really and truly."

"Really and truly? My brother, definitely. I wanted to be just like him. I even dressed like a boy, for a while."

Millicent was surprised to learn that Mrs. Taylor had gone to such lengths to be the favorite in her family. "Did it work?"

"No. I grew older and found other things to occupy myself." She smiled. "When I think back on it, it was rather silly of me to run around wearing my brother's clothes, trying to be a boy so my parents would like me best."

Millicent thought so, too. She had already decided there was a better way to become the family favorite. Being helpful. She would make herself — what was the word? Indispensable. Her parents wouldn't be able to do without her. Her mother and father would get up in the morning and say, first thing, "Where is Millicent? We can't make a single decision without Millicent. We're lost without her."

"Millicent, dear, it's getting dark outside," Mrs. Taylor said gently. "You and Rudy better go before your parents worry."

Millicent tucked Jocko under her arm and told Rudy to put his jacket on. "Thanks for the tea. It was fun."

"Thank you for bringing the paper. I enjoy it very much." Mrs. Taylor walked them to the door and watched until they were safely down the hill.

It was too late to try to sell the extra copy of the *Wagner Avenue Chronicle.* Maybe she could sell it tomorrow, at half price, the way the grocery store sold day-old bread.

"Daddy's here!" Rudy shrieked, running into the house ahead of Millicent.

Millicent saw her father's car in the driveway behind Abby's yellow car and her mother's station wagon. Her father was home late from his job at the Labor Department in Washington, D.C.

Everyone was gathered in the kitchen.

"Hi, Daddy," Millicent said. She waved to her mother, who was on the phone.

"Hi, kids." Mr. Adams tugged a lock of Millicent's hair and gave Rudy a mock punch on the arm. Then he began sorting through the mail on the kitchen counter. His hair was windblown because he never wore a hat. His bald spot seemed even balder.

Abby was perched on the stool, peeling carrots. "Don't be so down on middle age," she said to her father, obviously continuing a discussion that had been interrupted by Millicent's and Rudy's noisy arrival. "My anthropology teacher says it's one of life's great stages."

Millicent rolled her eyes. Ever since Abby started going to George Mason University last fall, she talked about her anthropology teacher all the time. Millicent didn't know what anthropology was, until Abby loftily explained that it was a course about the study of the human race. Millicent pictured Abby and the other students running around the classroom every day.

Mr. Adams didn't think much of Abby's anthropology teacher. "What does your teacher know about middle age? He's still wet behind the ears."

Millicent giggled. Apparently Abby's teacher didn't own any towels.

Abby finished the carrot and wiped her hands. "He's not wet behind the ears. He's twenty-seven. Anyway, you don't have to be dead to know about graveyards."

"I suppose your teacher thinks that's another of life's great stages?" Mr. Adams said wryly.

Abby flounced off the stool. "Honestly. There's no talking to you when you're in this mood."

Mr. Adams smiled. "That's what happens when you hit middle age. You get cranky."

As her older sister swept by, tall and smart-looking, Millicent was struck by the difference in their ages. Abby was seventeen, almost eighteen. And Geneva, the oldest sister, was twenty-two. According to Millicent's grandmother Helena, her parents had had two families. First Geneva and Abigail, and then, years later, Millicent and Rudy.

Mrs. Adams once jokingly remarked that she and her husband had the longest memberships in the PTA of anyone they knew. "I'll be a room mother forever," she'd added with a laugh.

Remembering what Mrs. Taylor had said about her brother being the favorite because he was the oldest, Millicent realized that Abby and Geneva were pretty tough competition for the favorite-child position. She would have to work very hard at being helpful to outshine those two.

"I'm going in my study," Mr. Adams said, wearily, Millicent thought. "Let your mother know, when she gets off the phone."

Millicent wondered why her father spent so much time lately in the little room off the kitchen. It used to be Abby's bedroom, back when Geneva was still living at home. After Geneva went away to college, Abby moved into her sister's old room and Mr. Adams converted the little room into a study. He put up bookshelves to hold his history books, and laid down a maroon rug Mrs. Adams said was hideous but Millicent thought was beautiful.

Usually her father went to his room after supper to read quietly and escape from "infernal machines," as he called the television and the telephone. He hated television, except for the news and educational programs. He didn't like the telephone either. "One numbs the brain and the other never lets you eat dinner in peace," he once remarked after answering the phone four times during dinner.

Her mother used the phone a lot these days, talking about the playground and other PTA business and also to take orders for her food co-op. And the TV was always tuned to a music video channel or cartoons. Maybe that was why her father ducked into his study, to get away from the racket.

Millicent wandered into the dining room. She was hungry, but it would be quite a while before they had supper. Maybe she could do something to speed things up. She could set the table, at least. That was helpful.

First she cleared the junk off the table, her school knapsack, Abby's anthropology textbook, several of Rudy's Matchbox cars, a strange drawing on funny blue paper.

Millicent studied the picture. Her mother's name was at the top. PTA business, probably. The picture showed a box with squiggly shapes around it. The shapes sort of resembled bushes. The bushes were terrible; even Rudy could draw better than that. If her mother showed the picture to the PTA people, they would fall over laughing.

Poor Mom, Millicent thought. Her mother could do lots of things, including fix the cars when they broke down, but she couldn't draw worth beans. Here was Millicent's first helpful assignment!

Taking her marking pens from her knapsack, Millicent sat down to redraw the picture. She made the squiggly lines into fantastic flowers, red and orange and pink, and colored a thick carpet of grass. She added a nice, round, yellow sun in the right-hand corner. The drawing looked a hundred percent better. Her mother would be so grateful, she'd probably declare Millicent her favorite child on the spot.

Just then Mrs. Adams came in from the kitchen. She was scribbling in a notebook. "I think I bit off more than I can chew with this playground project. It seemed so easy when they asked me to head the committee."

"Look, Mom," Millicent chirped. "I fixed your drawing. Now nobody'll laugh at it."

Her mother dropped the notebook and rushed over. "You fixed my — oh no! Millicent! You colored all over my blueprint!"

"Blueprint?" Millicent echoed. "What's a blueprint?"

Mrs. Adams frantically scraped at the yellow sun. "*This* is a blueprint. It's a sketch of the new playground I was going to take to the architect's tomorrow. The committee finally approved it. From this sketch, the architect will draw up the final plans. And this ink is *not* coming off."

Millicent's heart dropped to her toenails. "You don't like what I did? Your bushes were awful, so I made them pretty, with flowers."

"The bushes aren't supposed to be pretty. They're landscape symbols — those squiggles represent the *idea* of a bush, so the landscape people will know we want a bush planted in that spot."

"Oh." Millicent felt awful. Here she'd tried to be helpful and she'd ruined her mother's picture. "I'm sorry, Mom. I didn't mean to mess it up. I thought I was helping, honest."

Her mother sighed. "I know you did. But, Millicent, what have I told you about bothering other people's things without asking?"

Millicent was anxious to repair the damage. "Do you have any more of this funny blue paper? I'll draw your picture the way you had it."

"Architectural drawing is hard. It took me forever just to get the school in the right place. I'll have to do it myself, Millicent." She glanced at the clock on the wall. "If I hurry supper, I'll have time to redraw it tonight."

"Can I do anything to help? Sharpen your pencils? Sweep the eraser crumbs?"

"No, thanks, Millicent. You've done quite enough already." Her mother went back into the kitchen to fix supper.

Millicent stared forlornly at the messed-up blueprint. She certainly wouldn't win her *mother's* vote for favorite child. Least favorite, maybe.

There was always her father. One good thing about having two parents — if she didn't gain the favor of one, she still had another parent to win over.

# 3

"We have to shut down the presses," Millicent said dramatically one morning as she and Roberta walked to school. "I hate to do it, but I don't have time to type the paper every day. Not since school started again."

To be truthful, Millicent was tired of the *Wagner Avenue Chronicle*. It was a big job being a newspaper mogul. And Millicent was doing more and more of the work. Roberta kept finding excuses not to help.

"We didn't make that much money anyway," Roberta said, as they crossed the field between Wagner Avenue and the Maple Hills development.

"Three dollars. That's not so bad."

"Yeah, but we each only got half of that. A dollar fifty isn't much money," Roberta argued. "I get more than that for my allowance."

Millicent knew Roberta received two dollars every Saturday. Plus, she got a dollar for every A on her report card. Millicent received an allowance, too, although not as much as Roberta's, but she didn't earn any money on her report card. Her father didn't believe in paying for good grades.

"Going to school and doing your best is your job," he told her once when she wanted to know why she couldn't have a dollar for her A in spelling. "Just like going to work at the Labor Department downtown is my job."

"But you get paid," Millicent pointed out.

"Knowledge is its own reward," her father said, in that infuriating way grown-ups had of using words to suit their purpose. "I hate to see you trying to get A's just for money."

She couldn't do it anyway, so her father needn't have worried about her emptying their savings account. She made A's in reading and spelling and that was it. Math was a real struggle — she was lucky to get a C.

Roberta made good grades without any apparent effort. She earned five or six dollars on every report card. Roberta's parents thought she was the smartest person to come along since Albert Einstein. If Roberta knew she was smart, she didn't act it but she *was* stubborn and sometimes hard to get along with.

If Millicent was the jealous type, she would have hated Roberta Holloway.

Besides being smart and an adopted only child, Roberta was cute. Everybody said so. Millicent's mother often remarked that Roberta was "made cute," which meant she wasn't all arms and legs like Millicent. Millicent was the tallest girl in their class. When they posed for their class picture last fall, Millicent had to sit beside the teacher, so she wouldn't tower over the other students. Roberta posed in the very center of the front row, and the rest of the class fanned out around her.

Still, they were best friends. Millicent thought their differences made life interesting. It was only when they clashed that there was trouble.

Which was one reason why Millicent decided to quit the newspaper business. Roberta was bored with it and they would only fight if Millicent tried to get Roberta to do her share.

The other reason for scrapping the paper was more important, at least to Millicent. If she wanted to become the favorite child in her family, she would have to focus all her energies toward that goal.

As they headed up the broad front steps of Green Acres Elementary, someone brushed by Millicent, nearly knocking her over.

"Sorry, Millie," a boy yelled.

"Bruce Johnston!" Millicent gasped, stooping to pull up a knee sock. "I should have known. Walk slow. Let him get ahead of us."

Bruce Johnston was in their class. He'd been in Millicent's class since first grade. Bruce's best friend was a new boy named Lorenzo Scrementi. They both lived in the Maple Hills development. Lorenzo was okay, but Bruce was impossible.

Last year Millicent sort of liked Bruce, until he pushed her off the monkey bars and made her skin her elbow. At the beginning of fourth grade, Millicent decided she couldn't stand him. But now, halfway into the year, she was changing her mind about Bruce again. She was afraid she really *did* like him. How could she like anybody who was always running into her and calling her "Millie," a nickname she despised?

In Room 6, Millicent sat down at the desk next to Roberta's. They'd picked seats across from each other so they could pass notes and whisper. Bruce sat in front of Millicent. Lorenzo Scrementi was already in his seat in front of Roberta.

After calling the roll, Mrs. Stann went to the board and wrote in big letters, "My Special Place." Setting the chalk back in the tray, she explained their assignment.

"I want you to write a paragraph about a place that is very special to you. A special place can be anywhere, as long as it is special to you. It can be your grandmother's house, a place you went to on vacation with your family, or even a place in your own backyard."

Bruce raised his hand. "A paragraph can be just two sentences, right?"

"Don't worry about length. I want you to write about how you really *feel* about this place. And then I would like you to draw a picture of your special place. Your essays and drawings will be displayed on the bulletin board outside the main office."

Mrs. Stann gave a stack of drawing paper to

Stacey Morrison, who was paper monitor for the week. Stacey was paper monitor nearly every week because she was the teacher's favorite. As Stacey smugly dropped a sheet of paper on Millicent's desk, Millicent decided that more than ever she wanted to feel favored, like Stacey. She'd convince her father that very night that she was indispensable. He would make her his favorite on the spot.

But first she had to complete the assignment Mrs. Stann had just given them. Beside her, Roberta was writing fast in her notebook.

"Have you thought of a place?" Millicent whispered.

Roberta nodded. "Disney World. I've been there three times."

Millicent hadn't been to Disney World, or to Colorado, like Roberta. Roberta had lots of special places to write about. Still, Mrs. Stann didn't say they could only write about faraway places. Just someplace special. What could she write about?

She peeked over Bruce's shoulder. In his messy script, Bruce was describing his favorite place, Wild World. He talked to Lorenzo as he scribbled.

"The wave machine is cool, but I really love the water slides," he said, mimicking a watery splash as he glided his pencil down an imaginary slide.

Lorenzo's paper was angled so Millicent could read it. *My favorite place is Radford College*, he'd written. *My cousin Elizabeth goes there and I went to visit her. All these kids were having fun in the halls and there was some funny stuff, like a Santa hot-line phone.*

Millicent had visited Abby's college, George Mason University, but it wasn't very special, at least not to her. And the one time she went to Wild World, she didn't like it. The wave machine made her seasick and the water slide scared her.

Her chin on her fist, she gazed out the window, hoping for inspiration. Against the blue sky the bare branches of a huge maple tree stood out in sharp clean lines.

Millicent loved looking at that tree. In the fall the maple was a splendor of scarlet foliage. And in the spring she watched new leaves unfold every day. When the weather was nice, Millicent often sat under the maple tree during recess.

Suddenly she knew what she could write about. The maple tree! The maple tree was as special to Millicent as his cousin's college was to Lorenzo. Or Wild World was to Bruce.

Now that she had a topic, she wrote a paragraph and then drew a picture of the maple tree.

Mrs. Stann collected their compositions and drawings. As she picked up Millicent's, she smiled. "That's the tree in the schoolyard," she commented with delight. "How wonderful that part of our school is your special place."

Bruce turned around to make a face, but Millicent ignored him. She was proud of her paper.

She hoped Mrs. Stann would put hers right in the center of the bulletin board.

"I'm going to clean Daddy's study," Millicent told her mother, waving a dust rag.

"That's nice," Mrs. Adams said absently, deep in paperwork.

Millicent went into her father's private room and closed the door. The idea of cleaning his room came to her on the way home from school that day. She would surprise her father with a sparkling, tidy room. Then he'd realize how indispensable she was. "I can't find a thing without Millicent," he'd declare helplessly. In no time, she'd be his favorite.

Actually, her father's room wasn't really dirty. Mrs. Adams cleaned it weekly and Abby ran the vacuum on Saturdays. Millicent flicked the dust rag over her father's books. There must be a million of them, jammed in floor-to-ceiling bookcases. Well, if not a million, easily a thousand or two.

She glanced at a couple of titles. *Life of the Celts*. *The Oxford History of Britain*. The Oxford history book was tall and thick. It practically hid the thinner book on Celts, whatever they were. Millicent stepped back from the bookcase. Her father's books seemed to be stuck on the shelves higgledy-piggledy. Big ones next to small ones. Thin books squeezed next to thick books. They weren't in alphabetical order, either. The big Oxford book was beside the Celt book. Millicent knew O did not come before C. How did her father ever find anything?

Millicent knew how she could help her father. She would rearrange his books by size! She'd put the small books at the top of the shelves, and the big heavy books on the bottom of the shelves, with the medium books in the middle. Her father's bookcases would look so much neater.

Humming, Millicent started pulling books off the shelves. Soon the maroon rug was littered with books. She made three rows: big books, medium-sized books, and little books. There were so many books, the stacks covered the floor. Some of the piles teetered dangerously.

Putting the books back was more difficult than tearing them off the shelves, she found. She couldn't reach the top shelves without standing on her father's desk. She had to keep jumping down for a new pile of small books. Rudy would have been glad to help hand her books, but Millicent had to do this all by herself. If Rudy helped, then he would get half the credit and Millicent wouldn't seem quite so indispensable.

After working an hour, Millicent glanced back down at the floor. There were more books than ever! She hadn't even touched the medium-sized books yet. And she was tired. Her legs hurt from springing up and down on the desk with an armload of heavy books. If only there were a simpler way.

She sat down on the desk and studied the last

three stacks of small books. These books were old, with crumbling bindings. They smelled funny, not like library books. She didn't know why her father kept such awful-looking books. Maybe she could throw them up on the shelves, one at a time, and then arrange them all at once. That would save a lot of time and it couldn't hurt the books any since they were already pretty beat-up.

Reaching down, she grabbed several books. Then she pitched a red volume above her head. Bingo! The book landed on the shelf. She threw another. That one missed, tumbling back down on the desk. She picked it up and aimed again. About half the books she tossed landed on the shelf the first time. Still, it was much quicker than clambering up and down on the desk.

The door to her father's study opened just as Millicent threw the last book, which missed. The book hit the desk with a dull thwack the instant Millicent saw her father standing in the door. His face was a mottled red.

"What are you doing, young lady?" he demanded, wading into the room. He tripped over a stack of medium-sized books. "Millicent! What is going on?"

She slid off the desk. "I'm rearranging your books, Daddy. They looked so messy, stuck on the shelves any old way. So I took them down and now I'm putting them back by size. See, the littlest books are on the top."

"By size! You can't arrange books by size!" He

glared at her. "What were you doing, throwing that book?"

"Uh — I got tired of climbing up on your desk, so I threw a few of them up there. Just the old, crummy-looking ones," she hastily amended. "They aren't much good."

"My first editions! I don't even read them unless my hands are clean and you threw them around like tennis balls. Millicent, I — " He looked furious and then all the anger seemed to deflate from him, like air from a balloon.

Mrs. Adams came to the door. Taking in the piles of books, she said, "What happened?"

"Millicent decided to rearrange my books," Mr. Adams replied wearily.

"Oh, Millicent." Mrs. Adams put her hands on her hips. "What have I told you about getting into people's things without asking them?"

"I couldn't ask Daddy. He wasn't here. Anyway, it was supposed to be a surprise."

"It was a surprise all right," Mr. Adams said.

"Daddy, you came in before I was finished. It'll look really neat. Just let me finish. I won't throw any more books, I promise. I'll carry them one by one, even if it takes me all night. And I'll wear gloves!"

He picked up a weighty, purple book. "I appreciate your thoughtfulness, Millicent, but I would rather not have my books arranged by size. I had them arranged by category. A system I made up. I knew exactly where everything was.

And now — thanks to you — I can't find a thing."

She winced. Those weren't *exactly* the words she'd imagined her father saying.

"I'll help you put them back the way you had them," she offered, eager to make things right again. "You just sit there and tell me where they go. I'll do all the work. You won't have to lift a finger."

"The books are too mixed up. It'll take me days to sort through them. Only I can do it." He sighed heavily.

Mrs. Adams touched Millicent's shoulder. "I think you'd better come with me. Your father can think better when he's alone." She led Millicent into the kitchen.

"I was only trying to do something nice for him," Millicent said plaintively. "I didn't mean to make him mad."

"Your father isn't mad," Mrs. Adams said. "He's just a little down in the dumps these days, that's all."

"He is? Why is he down in the dumps?"

"Oh, things," her mother replied vaguely.

Millicent tried to think what things might be bothering her father. "Is he down in the dumps because of his old bald spot?" Maybe she shouldn't have written about her father's newly discovered bald spot in the *Wagner Avenue Chronicle*. He wasn't thrilled about it, she recalled.

Her mother smiled. "Oh, no, honey. He was a little sensitive about his bald spot at first, but he's over it now. It's nothing for you to worry about."

Despite her mother's reassurances, Millicent *was* worried about her father. Down in the dumps certainly described the way he'd been acting lately. Taking long walks alone. Spending hours in the study. She couldn't get the picture of her father sitting on a heap of trash in the city dump out of her mind.

Here was a way she could truly be helpful. She would find out what was bothering her father and fix it. Then he wouldn't be mad at her any more for messing up his books.

I can do it, Millicent silently resolved. She would save her father from whatever was making him sad. The whole family would be so grateful, she'd be *everybody's* favorite. They might even name a special day after her.

She could see it on the calendar now, marked in red. Millicent T. Adams Day. A day to celebrate.

# 4

"I wish the baby shower were today," Millicent said, as she finished coloring the last page shaped like a baby bottle.

"It's only another week," Abby said, stapling the pages into a booklet. There was a pile of bottle-shaped booklets in the middle of the table. Half of the booklets were colored pink, half blue.

"I know. But I still wish it were today." Millicent was forever wishing her life away, according to her mother. When it was Thanksgiving, she couldn't wait until Christmas. When Christmas rolled around, she was anxious for it to be Valentine's Day. As early as April she began counting the days until school was out for the year.

Geneva's baby shower was Millicent's first grown-up party. The night before her mother had taken her shopping so she could buy Geneva's shower present. Millicent lingered over the soft, white teddy bears and wooly lambs, half-wanting to buy one for herself, but they cost too much. She settled on a hooded bath towel printed with bunnies. She wrapped the present herself in left-over Christmas paper, tying a yellow rattle to the red bow. She thought that touch was very original.

"I'm going to be an aunt," she said as if she suddenly realized that fact. "And I'm only nine years old." Her aunt Pat was a lot older than nine. She was at least thirty or forty, ancient, really.

Rudy skated into the kitchen in his sock-feet. "So? I'm going to be an uncle and I'm only seven. I'm a younger uncle than you are an aunt."

Millicent stared at him. That was quite a mouthful for a second-grader. Sometimes her brother surprised her.

He picked up one of the booklets. "A baby bottle book! That's cute." Slowly he read, " 'How many words can you make from N-E-W B-A-B-Y?' "

"Put that down, Rudy." Millicent took the booklet out of his hands. "We're not supposed to do the games before next Saturday. That's cheating."

"We can't play them anyway." Abby divided the pink and blue game booklets, eight of each.

"I know," Millicent said. "We're helping Mom and Geneva's friend. So we're — what's the word?"

"Disqualified. We'll be too busy to play games," Abby stated. "This is a big party."

Rudy hung on the back of Abby's chair. "Can I go? I want to go to Geneva's bath party."

"Shower," Millicent corrected. "Not bath."

Abby smiled at him. "Afraid not, Rudy. This shower is just for women."

Rudy half-twisted around to stare accusingly at

Millicent. "Millicent's going and she's not a woman."

"I am, too," Millicent argued. "Practically."

"Roberta's going and she's not a woman either," Rudy said.

Abby laughed. "Well, women and girls. Don't forget, Dad is taking you and Craig to a basketball game next Saturday. You'll have fun, too."

But not as much fun as we'll have, Millicent thought. Even more important than being invited to a grown-up party, Millicent was to be a helper.

"Mom said I could mix the punch. And we have to make fifty tiny little sandwiches. Fifty!" Seeing her brother's crestfallen expression, she added kindly, "I'll bring you a piece of cake, Rudy. It's supposed to be shaped like a stork. What part do you want?"

Rudy scratched his ear. Millicent figured he wasn't quite sure what a stork looked like, but he knew it was some kind of a big bird. "The beak," he said finally. "Bring me the beak part." Happy again, he ran into the living room to watch TV.

Except for the murmur of the television set, the house was quiet. Millicent's parents were out running errands. Abby was watching Millicent and Rudy and for once, nobody was fighting or bickering. It was very peaceful, the kind of afternoon that made Millicent glad she was a member of her family, living in the brick bungalow on Wagner Avenue. If a stranger came in, he would think everything was perfect.

But Millicent knew it wasn't. Not really.

Elaborately gathering up the paper scraps, Millicent casually asked her sister, "What's wrong with Daddy these days? He seems . . . down in the dumps."

"He is," Abby replied readily.

"Is it because of his bald spot?"

Abby shook her head. "It's more serious than that, Mil. Daddy was passed over at work."

Millicent didn't know what being passed over meant. "Is that like not being promoted to the next grade?"

"Something like that. Being passed over means he thought he was getting a better job, but somebody else was given it instead. I heard Mom and Dad talking the other night. I'm pretty sure that's why he's been acting so down lately." Abby sighed. "My anthropology teacher would say Daddy is probably having a mid-life crisis. It's very common at his age."

Millicent thought about this. A mid-life crisis! At last she knew why her father was down in the dumps, but she didn't know how she'd ever help him. How could she help her father get the better job?

Last year Rudy had nearly failed first grade, which was something like being passed over at work. Mr. and Mrs. Adams went to Rudy's room at school for a parent-teacher conference. They reviewed Rudy's schoolwork and decided to help Rudy with his reading so he wouldn't fail.

Maybe she could go to her father's office and talk to his boss, have a daughter-boss conference. She pictured herself riding the subway downtown to Washington, D.C., marching into her father's boss's office, and demanding to see a folder of her father's latest paperwork.

"I don't know how to help him," she said.

Abby bundled the baby shower booklets with a rubber band. "I don't think any of us can help him. Maybe he just needs somebody to talk to. Daddy keeps to himself a lot. Talking might help."

Talking was something Millicent was especially good at. Her teacher even commented on Millicent's last report card that Millicent "enjoyed chatting with her neighbors."

As soon as he came home, she would have a private talk with her father.

But when her parents were home later that afternoon, they were busy. Her mother had phone calls to make, and hot rolls to bake and freeze for Geneva's shower. Her father had to go back to the hardware store to buy a putty knife he forgot when he was there earlier. Rudy went with him, so Millicent didn't have the opportunity to have her private chat. She stayed home and helped her mother make rolls.

The rolls took a long time. By the time Millicent and her mother had cleaned up the floury kitchen, it was six-thirty. Mrs. Adams wanted to fix a simple supper, like beans and franks. Abby said she'd rather send out for a pizza. Millicent seconded her sister's suggestion. Mrs. Adams said they had eaten out the night before when they went shopping and couldn't afford it two nights in a row, not even pizza. Mr. Adams said he was hungry and wanted *real* food.

So they had hamburgers for dinner, one of Millicent's favorites, and kale, which she wasn't so crazy about. The kale was one of Mrs. Adams' food co-ops bargains. Whenever she found produce at a fair price, she bought enough for everyone on their street, with a lot left over for the residents of 9109 Wagner Avenue. Millicent wondered, as she struggled to swallow a strand of the icky stuff, why her mother's bargains were always apt to be green and yucky, never anything yummy like Twinkies.

Everyone seemed to be irritable by the time dinner was served. It was after seven and they were all tired and hungry. Rudy whimpered that he wanted beans and franks, not this green stuff, and Abby said she planned to buy herself a pizza anyway when she went to the library. Mrs. Adams said she wished she had a maid, even if only for half an hour, and Mr. Adams told her she had taken on too many outside activities.

Millicent wasn't worried that her parents would get into an argument because they never did. They had *discussions* from time to time, but never arguments.

"We're all out of sorts," Mrs. Adams said, getting up to clear the table. "It's the mid-winter blahs, I guess."

"I'm not out of sorts, Mom," Millicent said.

"Well, you're the only one, then. Help me with these dishes. You too, Rudy. Abby, don't be too late."

Abby stood at the door, looking at her family with a sad expression. "I don't know how I'll get a decent grade on my anthropology paper," she lamented. "This family is just too dull to write about."

Millicent knew her sister was referring to a big report she had to write. Abby was supposed to pretend she was a scientist visiting from the future. She had to figure out what kind of people once lived in their house, like those scientists who studied Egyptian temples — archeologists.

Millicent thought the report sounded fun, but Abby rolled her eyes with despair every time she mentioned the assignment.

"If only you weren't so *ordinary*," she said tragically. "How can I pretend I'm discovering the ruins of a fascinating civilization with all this stuff around like Matchbox cars?"

Mr. Adams picked up the scattered sections of the *Washington Post* strewn on the coffee table. "Maybe you can rent a family more interesting than ours."

"Very funny." Abby buttoned her coat and left in a huff.

Mrs. Adams chuckled. "She wants to impress

her teacher so much. Well, kids, these dishes aren't doing themselves."

Mr. Adams headed into his study with the paper. "This is all I have to read, now that the *Wagner Avenue Chronicle* presses have shut down."

"I didn't know you missed it," Millicent said with surprise.

"Where else could I read about my own bald spot?" He disappeared into his room.

Millicent helped her mother load the dishwasher, then she rapped on her father's study door. It was time to have that private talk.

"Come in."

Her father was leaning back in his shabby easy chair, his eyes closed, the newspaper abandoned on the hassock.

Millicent sat cross-legged on the maroon rug and looked around. All the books were back the way they were before she decided to arrange them by size.

"How come you're not reading your paper?" she asked.

Without opening his eyes, Mr. Adams replied, "I glanced at the local headlines. The county supervisor is making stupid decisions again, so I stopped reading. I don't know how such a nincompoop ever got voted into office."

Millicent dimly recalled that her father hadn't voted in the last election. Usually he was interested in such things and he always took her and

Rudy with him to the polls. Millicent and Rudy stood guard outside the curtained booth while their father voted. But this year, Mr. Adams had not gone to Green Acres Elementary to vote.

Millicent said, "If you don't like this guy, you should have voted for the one you liked. Maybe he would have won instead."

Mr. Adams snorted. "I didn't like anybody on the ballot. They were both idiots." He sighed. "The way things are these days, one person can't make a difference anymore, so why bother voting?"

Millicent was puzzled. "What do you mean, one person can't make a difference anymore?"

"Well, in the past — " Her father often began his sentences with that phrase. He was a history buff and loved to read about the olden days. "In the past," he repeated, "individuals were able to make outstanding contributions. Some of them literally changed the world."

"Like who?" Millicent was still confused. Sometimes it was hard to follow her father's conversations.

"Abraham Lincoln," he intoned. "Martin Luther King. Franklin D. Roosevelt. Those men did things that changed the world and the way we think."

"What about women? Didn't they change the world, too?"

"They certainly did. Eleanor Roosevelt was a

wonderful First Lady. She made this world a better place to live."

Millicent didn't know who Eleanor Roosevelt was. "How about Walt Disney?" she said, contributing the only famous name she could think of.

Her father smiled. "Yes, Walt Disney definitely made the world a better place to live. Especially in Florida and California." Then he became serious again. "But I wonder if we'll ever have any more individuals like Walt Disney and Eleanor Roosevelt. One person can't make a difference these days."

"Why not?"

"The world is a different place now, Millicent. Things are more complicated. In this day and age, it'd take a miracle to make real changes."

Miracle. Millicent tasted the word on her tongue. A miracle! At last she knew how to help her father. One person *could* make a difference.

She didn't quite follow everything her father said, but she knew now how to help him climb out of the dumps. In only a day, two at the most, she would be the unanimous choice for family favorite, elected in a landslide for making her father happy again. Everyone would be so grateful to her. Especially her father.

Her father needed a miracle. And she — Millicent T. Adams — was going to give him one.

# 5

On the way to school Monday morning, Millicent explained her plan to Roberta.

"The only way to get Daddy out of the dumps is to show him a miracle," she concluded. "I don't mind making one, but I'm not sure what one is."

"You don't know what a miracle is?" Roberta asked.

Millicent hated to admit total ignorance. "Sure, I've heard the *word* before . . . Abby will say it'll be a miracle if she passes her English course. Or Daddy will come home and say it's a miracle he made it, because of the traffic on the Beltway. But what *is* a miracle?"

"Let's look it up in the dictionary in the library," Roberta suggested.

"Good idea." Millicent believed the answers to just about every question were to be found somewhere in the library.

"Isn't this warm weather great?" Roberta said. "We'll get to play outside today."

It was very warm for January. Millicent had left her stocking cap and mittens at home on the chair by the door. Roberta wasn't wearing her stocking cap either, but she did have a cherry-colored muffler wound around her neck. Mrs. Holloway worried constantly about Roberta's health. If Roberta so much as sniffled, Mrs. Holloway rushed her to the doctor.

Now Roberta defiantly tugged the scarf free. Millicent went one step further and unzipped her jacket. It felt like spring.

"We'll play outside all week if it stays this warm," Millicent said. "I hate sharing the cafeteria with the little kids." Whenever it was cold or rainy, the fourth-graders had recess in the cafeteria with the third-graders.

Just then Sheila and Craig Sanders, with Rudy in tow, zoomed past them on the sidewalk.

"We'll beat you!" Rudy called good-naturedly.

"Fourth-graders are so *slow*," Sheila jeered.

Millicent made a face, but Sheila had already run ahead. "It's hard to believe we were that dumb, just last year."

"We weren't ever *that* dumb," Roberta declared.

At Green Acres Elementary, Millicent and Roberta went straight to the library. Millicent made a beeline for the huge dictionary and quickly flipped the tissue-thin pages to the M section. She had to force herself not to look at any of the tiny colored pictures or read any other definitions. Dictionaries were as fascinating as maps — she could pore over them for hours.

Roberta spied the word first. "Here it is. 'Miracle: an extremely outstanding or unusual event. A thing of wonder that cannot be explained.' "

" 'An unusual event,' " Millicent repeated musingly. "Like spring in January, I guess. And rainbows."

"No, it has to be something that *can't* be explained," Roberta said. "Rainbows can be explained. We learned about them in science, remember? The light hits the raindrops a certain way and — "

"Rainbows seem like a miracle to me," Millicent disagreed. "How about spring in January? You can't explain that."

"Yes, you can. My father says it happens all the time, warm weather in winter. It's called a January thaw or something. My father says it's caused by a wave of warm air from the South. When a wave of cold air comes back, it'll be winter again."

Millicent was sick of hearing what Roberta's father said all the time. *Her* father said very little these days, because he was so far down in the dumps. She needed a miracle to dig him out and she needed one fast.

"I have to think of a miracle," she stated. "It's the only way I can help my father."

Roberta jabbed the dictionary with her index finger. "It says right there a miracle is something you can't really explain. Something nobody's ever seen before."

"How can I make something nobody's ever seen before?" Millicent asked as they left the library. "It'll be tough enough trying to make something people *have* seen before, like spring in January."

"Are you sure this is the only thing that will help your father? Can't you just make him a funny card or maybe some brownies?"

"It has to be a miracle. He told me so himself. I'll think of something, don't worry." Millicent spoke with more confidence than she felt. She had no idea how she was going to dream up an unusual or outstanding event to help her father believe that one person — namely, Millicent — could make a difference in the world. If she wanted to be elected family favorite, she had to come up with an original miracle.

They walked slowly down the hall. Millicent hoped an idea would flash over her head, like light-bulb ideas in cartoons.

Mrs. Stann bustled past them, carrying a stack of freshly printed mimeographs. "The tardy bell is about to ring, girls. No lollygagging in the halls."

Millicent giggled. Sometimes her teacher said the funniest things!

"No lollygagging, Millie," a familiar voice mimicked. A hand tugged the belt of her jacket, dragging her backwards.

"Stop it, Bruce!" Millicent yelled. She jerked free and whirled around.

Bruce Johnston grinned at her. Lorenzo Scrementi was with him, as always.

Lorenzo smiled apologetically at Millicent. He was okay, she thought. Too bad Bruce didn't take lessons from his friend.

Millicent walked backwards the rest of the way to Room 6. She didn't trust Bruce behind her. He'd probably step on her heels or pull her hair.

After the Pledge of Allegiance, Mrs. Stann asked Stacey Morrison to pass out the mimeographs. Once again Millicent wondered what it was like to always be chosen, to be the favored one. She was going to a lot of trouble to be the favorite in her family — creating a miracle to cheer up her father. All Stacey had to do was erase the blackboard.

Thinking up a new miracle was hard. Miracles didn't just fall out of the sky into a person's lap. Millicent took out a sheet of notebook paper. Her mother made lists all the time — PTA lists, playground committee lists, food co-op lists. Millicent decided to make a list of miracles she thought she could do.

"We're going to be starting a new unit," Mrs. Stann was saying, interrupting Millicent's concentration. "About Rome. We'll learn about Roman mythology, the way Romans lived and ate and dressed. As you can see on the mimeograph, these are the topics we will cover and the tests we will have."

Millicent glanced briefly at the mimeograph,

then returned to her list. She was more interested in miracles than Romans at the moment. Numbering one through ten on the paper, she hoped she wouldn't need ten miracles. One good miracle ought to do the trick.

In front of her, Bruce Johnston dropped his pencil. It landed near Millicent's left foot. When he bent to pick it up, he swiftly untied her shoelace.

Grinning, he straightened up and said, "Your shoe's untied. Sloppy, sloppy, Millie."

With a frown of annoyance, Millicent retied her tennis shoe.

"What's this?" Bruce said, still twisted around in his chair. He was staring at her list, headed "Miracles."

Millicent flipped the paper over. "Mind your own beeswax," she retorted.

"Does the teacher know you're not doing schoolwork?"

"Will you be quiet!" It was hard enough trying to think up ten miracles — or even one miracle — without Bruce Johnston bugging her.

"Bruce," Mrs. Stann said sharply. "Eyes front. You and Millicent stop that chattering. Pay attention, both of you."

Guiltily, Millicent slid her list in the cubby under her desk. Darn that Bruce. He talked to her first. And now Mrs. Stann was put out with *her*.

She listened to Mrs. Stann talk until recess

about life in Rome. As they followed their class outside, Roberta asked Millicent if she'd thought of a miracle yet.

"No," Millicent said dismally. "Being a miracle-maker is a lot tougher than being a newspaper mogul."

"If miracles were easy, then they wouldn't be miracles," Roberta said logically. "You want to play on the blacktop?"

Millicent wasn't interested in joining in the rowdy game of dodgeball. "Let's go around to the side yard where my tree is. I can think better away from all these kids."

They walked around the playground to the yard at the side of the building. Millicent's maple tree grew here, along with lots of other trees and bushes.

Millicent went over to sit under her maple tree while Roberta picked up spiny horse chestnuts from beneath a nearby horse chestnut tree.

"In case Bruce and Lorenzo try to bother us," she said. "Now we have some ammunition."

Millicent leaned her head against the trunk and looked up through the branches. Tiny purple buds were popping out on the branches — it had been that warm lately. Mrs. Stann had prominently displayed her "special place" essay and drawing of the maple tree in the very center of the bulletin board by the main office. Everyone who came into the school could stop and read her essay about the maple tree.

Too bad miracles didn't grow on trees, like the leaves, Millicent thought. She could reach up and pick one, that easily. Roberta was probably right. If miracles were commonplace, nobody would be impressed when one happened.

Then she noticed a drop of moisture clinging to a twig. A sunbeam speared the droplet. Millicent tracked the path of the ray to a utility door behind her. A shimmering rainbow danced on the white-painted metal door.

A rainbow. No matter what Roberta said, it seemed like a miracle to her, the way the sun shone through a plain old drop of water and made a wonderful band of colors. Miracles did grow on trees! she thought joyfully. There, on the door behind her, was the miracle that would cure her father's sadness.

Millicent went directly home after school. "Is Abby here?" she asked her mother.

"In her room," Mrs. Adams replied, steeped in paperwork for the playground project.

Millicent rapped on her sister's door. Abby was doing homework and listening to her stereo.

"Hey, kid. What's up?" Her sister never minded when Millicent came in her room.

"Can I borrow your glass earrings?" Millicent asked. "I only need them for a day. I promise I won't lose them."

"My glass earrings? Oh, you mean my crystal earrings. Sure, go ahead. They're in my jewelry box. Put them back when you're through."

Millicent found the crystal earrings in a tangle of necklaces and bracelets. "Thanks!"

In her own room, she put the earrings in the plastic hairclip tray on her dresser. It was too late in the day to perform her homemade miracle, but tomorrow morning would be perfect. *If* the sun was shining.

The next morning Millicent yanked her shade upward, before she even got out of bed. In a pool of pink-and-orange-tinted sky, the sun was just appearing over Mrs. Taylor's rooftop. Millicent bounded out of bed and ran out to the kitchen, clutching one of Abby's crystal earrings.

Her father was alone at the table, drinking coffee from the #1 Dad mug Millicent had given him for Christmas.

"Hi, Daddy," she said brightly.

He regarded her with surprise. "You're up early."

"I wanted to see you before you went to work." She sat down and studied her father gravely. "How are you today, Daddy?"

"How am I?" He lifted one eyebrow. "Did you get up just to inquire about my health?"

"Sort of." She figured that the miracle wouldn't have much effect if her father were feeling like his old self again. She watched him closely as he scanned the front page of the newspaper. He gave a discontented sigh. No, he wasn't better. The newspaper was making him sad.

"Bad news?" she asked hopefully.

"It's never good." He rinsed his cup in the sink. "Well, off to the salt mines."

The salt mines was what her father called his job lately. He was still down in the dumps. Her father definitely needed her miracle.

"Wait, Daddy." She jumped up from the table. "I want to show you something. Something really neat."

"Oh, pumpkin, I can't be late today. I have an eight-thirty meeting. Can it wait until tonight?"

"No, it can't." She ran over to the window and pushed the curtains back. Sunlight streamed through the glass. "It'll only take a second. And it'll be wonderful, you'll see."

Just then Rudy shuffled into the kitchen. His GI Joe pajamas were rumpled and his sandy hair stood up in spikes. "I thought I heard you guys talking," he said sleepily. "How come you're up so early, Millie?"

Rudy was the only person in the entire world she let call her "Millie." She truly loved her little brother. But she didn't need any distractions as she was about to perform her first miracle.

"I'm getting ready to show Daddy something," she said. "You can see it, too, if you sit down over there and be still."

Rudy hiked himself up on the tall stool. "What am I going to see?"

"Millicent — " Her father picked up his briefcase. "I really have to run."

"Look, Daddy!" Millicent positioned herself with the sun behind her and held up the dangling crystal earring. With shaking fingers, she aimed a sunray through the earring. Suppose it didn't work?

Magically, a wobbly band of colors appeared faintly on the opposite wall.

Rudy's jaw dropped. "Wow! Millie made a rainbow!"

"It's a miracle," Millicent said with relief. "Isn't it, Daddy? Don't you feel terrific, now that you've seen a miracle? And on an ordinary Tuesday morning, too!"

"It's very nice," Mr. Adams allowed. "But it's not really a miracle."

"Yes, it is!" she cried. Was her father so far gone he didn't recognize a miracle when it was right in front of him?

"Daddy, what's a miracle?" Rudy asked. "I thought it was a rainbow."

"It is a rainbow." Mr. Adams took the crystal earring from Millicent. He turned it so the rainbow on the wall was even more brilliant. "The earring acts as a prism. It refracts sunlight — splits it — and produces the rainbow. You see, white light is actually made up of colors, and this piece of glass separates each color as the light passes through it."

Rudy reached for the earring. "Can I make one?"

"No," Millicent snapped. "It's a miracle. Not just anybody can make one. Only a very special person can do it — "

"Daddy just did. I want to make one, too."

Mr. Adams handed the earring to Rudy. "Got to run. See you kids tonight." He ruffled Rudy's hair, then pecked Millicent on the cheek. "Thanks for the treat, pumpkin. I did enjoy it."

Millicent frowned as Rudy made weak rainbows on the wall. Some miracle, she thought sourly. It never occurred to her that her father knew how to make rainbows, too.

There was only one thing to do, she decided with a sigh. She'd have to come up with another miracle to make her father feel better.

A *real* one, this time.

# 6

On the morning of the baby shower, Millicent got up at six-fifteen and put on the new outfit her aunt Patricia gave her for Christmas. Then she skipped out to the kitchen, where her parents were slumped over their first cup of coffee. Abby was still in bed. Mrs. Adams and Abby had been up very late the night before, cooking for the party.

When her mother saw Millicent already dressed, she said, "The shower isn't until two o'clock this afternoon. That's — " On her fingers, she tried to count how many hours away that was, but it was too early even for simple arithmetic. "Change into your jeans," she told Millicent. "You can't run around all day in your good outfit."

"I won't get dirty," Millicent said. "I'll sit still until it's time to leave. I won't move a muscle." She sat stiffly, with her arms at her sides.

"You can't stay like a statue all day," Mr. Adams said.

Millicent relaxed. "I'm not an ordinary guest, you know. I'm a helper."

Roberta was coming with them. She was a party

helper, too. But Millicent would be the chief helper, she decided. After all, Geneva was her own sister. It was only right that Millicent, sister of the guest of honor, be the chief helper.

Until she thought of another miracle, being the best helper at Geneva's party was a way to become the family favorite.

She'd be such a good helper, her mother would surely brag to her father, "Millicent was wonderful. I counted on her to do everything." Her father would answer with deep admiration, "I'm not surprised. She's not our favorite child for nothing." Maybe her father would cheer up on the spot, not be down in the dumps any more, knowing that he could count on his favorite child.

At last it was time to leave for the party. Millicent, who had managed to keep her new outfit clean, was lacing the ribbons of her black ballet shoes when her mother came in her room.

"Oh, honey, you can't wear those shoes," she told Millicent. The soles are too thin. You'll catch cold."

The springlike weather had vanished. The temperature was freezing again, though there was still no sign of snow.

"But I don't have anything except my running shoes," Millicent protested. She loved her ballet shoes. They weren't real ballet slippers, just shoes with ribbons to hold them on her feet. "I don't want to wear sneakers."

"You'll have to. I don't want you getting sick."

The running shoes looked terrible with her pink wool plaid skirt and pink tights. Her ballet shoes were perfect. So what if it was a little cold?

Millicent clumped woodenly out to the kitchen.

"You look very nice," her mother remarked, taking foil-wrapped bowls from the refrigerator. "I made you a sandwich. You ought to eat before we go."

The doorbell rang twice, Roberta's signal.

"I'll get it! It's probably Roberta." Millicent ran to open the door.

Roberta stood on the porch, holding her baby shower gift. She had on her parka with the ski lift ticket still attached to the zipper. Millicent noticed Roberta was wearing a new skirt, too, but it was what Roberta had on her feet that filled Millicent with envy. Instead of clunky running shoes, Roberta wore short, green suede boots, the sort Robin Hood or Peter Pan would wear.

Millicent stepped back from the door, trying to hide her own feet. "Come in," she said. "We're almost ready."

Mrs. Adams deposited a box of napkins and paper plates by the door. "Hello, Roberta. Don't you look darling? Have you had lunch?"

Millicent's bubbly mood began to fizzle. Her mother didn't say *she* looked darling, only very nice. Who could look darling with those awful shoes she had to wear?

"I was too excited to eat," Roberta said. "My mother made me some soup, but I poured it down the sink when she wasn't looking."

"Millicent, I want you to eat a bite before we go," Mrs. Adams said before dashing back into the kitchen.

"You really ought to take that silly piece of paper off your jacket," Millicent said. Close up, Roberta's boots looked velvety soft. She longed to touch them.

Abby came in, dressed for the shower in a powder blue sweater and skirt. "Hi, kids. I'm packing the car. Any volunteers?"

"Me!" Millicent and Roberta both cried at the same time.

"Roberta can help me," Abby said.

Millicent frowned. "I said it first."

"You have to go eat," Mom said. "I'll take this box."

Abby pushed a smaller box toward Roberta. "You take that one if it's not too heavy."

"It's not heavy," Roberta said. "I'm strong." She hefted the heaviest box, staggering out the door with it.

As they went out to the car, Millicent heard Abby say, "By the way, I love your boots."

Roberta and her boots would get a lot of attention at the party, Millicent thought. People would ask Roberta why she had a piece of paper tied to her parka zipper, and they'd be impressed when Roberta told them she skied down the Bunny Slope in Colorado. Then they'd remark how cute Roberta was, with her shiny black hair and her green boots and her littleness. Nobody would pay any attention to brown-haired, too-tall Millicent.

Her mother had left a ham salad sandwich on a paper towel on the kitchen table. Rudy was eating his sandwich, swinging his legs.

"Daddy said Craig and I could have two hot dogs and two ice creams at the basketball game," he said.

"Just don't eat too much junk, please." Mrs. Adams carefully eased the molded salads she had made the night before into an ice chest. Shutting the lid, she left to make sure Abby was loading the car properly.

"The station wagon is packed to the roofrack," she muttered. "All those huge presents. I hope we have room for everything."

Millicent's father had already loaded Abby's present, a rocking chair, and an enormous carton containing a bassinet, the gift from her parents, in the car. There wasn't even room for a goldfish in the back.

Millicent peered into the ice chest. There was plenty of space for a pair of black ballet slippers. She ran to her room for her good shoes. The slippers fit nicely on top of the salads, nestled between the layers of foil her mother had used to cover the bowls. She closed the lid, smiling to herself. Roberta wouldn't be the only cute helper at the party.

Geneva and Lyman lived in Maryland, about thirty miles away. They both attended the University of Maryland. They had an apartment near the campus.

On the long drive around the Beltway, Millicent and Roberta played the license plate game. Millicent spied more out-of-state plates than Roberta, but Roberta claimed Millicent cheated.

"You can't count Maryland plates when we're in Virginia, or Virginia plates when we're in Maryland," Roberta insisted. "Or D.C. plates anywhere. They aren't really out of state."

"Sure they are," Millicent said airily. She kept her arm protectively around the ice chest wedged between them. "Mom asked me to help unmold the salads. You have to do it just right, or the design will be ruined." She said this in a tone that implied people who lifted heavy boxes were incapable of delicate tasks like unmolding fruit salads.

"Abby said I could help her put the presents in the bassinet," Roberta retaliated. "That's an important job, too."

"Not so important. Anybody can stack presents, but it takes an *expert* with steady hands to unmold salads." Millicent's entire future as family favorite depended on being the best, cutest helper at the party. She couldn't afford to be upstaged by Roberta, even if she was Millicent's best friend.

Soon they arrived at a big apartment complex. Millicent pointed to a red brick building. "Geneva and Lyman live there. Where's Lyman's car?" she asked her mother. "I don't see it."

"He was invited to the shower, but he decided this was really Geneva's day." She parked the car and they got out, each carrying a box or a bag up the single flight of stairs to Geneva's apartment.

A girl about Geneva's age let them in. "Hi, everybody. I'm Karen. Come on in."

The apartment bloomed with yellow and white decorations. Millicent admired the yellow paper umbrella suspended from the light fixture over the dining room table. When no one was watching, she swiped a fingerful of yellow frosting from the huge stork cake in the center of the table. She never could resist sampling fancy cake icing.

Geneva came out and hugged them. She wore her blue jumper with a new blouse. Her long blonde hair flowed loosely from a blue velvet headband. She looked beautiful and happy.

"The kitchen is a wreck," she told her mother cheerfully. "Pile things on the counter, if you can find room."

Mrs. Adams set Millicent to work immediately, not unmolding salads, as she had hoped, so she could demonstrate her delicate skill, but trimming the crusts off a million tea sandwiches Karen had made.

Roberta, the lucky, was arranging gifts in the lace-skirted bassinet in the living room. When the guests started arriving, Roberta answered the door and took coats. Millicent could hear Geneva's friends squealing over the cute door-opener. Roberta was stealing the show from Millicent before

Millicent could get on the stage. Nobody could see how cute *she* looked, stuck in the kitchen! Then she remembered her ballet slippers in the ice chest. She was still wearing her clumpy old running shoes.

At that moment, Mrs. Adams decided to unpack the molded salads. She lifted the lid of the chest and peeled back the first layer of foil. Her shriek bounced around the tiny kitchen.

"What *is* this!"

"Just my shoes." Millicent hurried over to retrieve her slippers. During the long jostling ride, her shoes had worked down under the foil. The toe of one slipper was stuck in the salmon mousse salad. When Millicent pulled it out, pinkish stuff dripped from her shoe onto the floor.

Mrs. Adams leaned against the counter, clutching her heart.

Roberta came in. "Oh, gross! Your smelly old shoes are in the *food*," she said in her loud voice. "*I'm* not eating any."

Millicent wiped her shoe clean with a paper towel. "Nobody will know the difference, unless somebody *tells*," she said meaningfully. "That part goes on the bottom. Right, Mom?"

Mrs. Adams had already dumped the salmon mousse into the garbage. "I think the others are OK. Millicent, whatever possessed you to put your shoes in my *salads?*"

Millicent wound the ribbons of her slippers around her ankles. "I didn't think it would hurt anything. Honest. It was the only place left to put them." She had tasted the salmon mousse and didn't feel it would be much of a loss. With her good shoes on, she was ready to show the guests that the chief helper was cute, too.

But her mother had other ideas. "Millicent, sprinkle dill on those pasta salads. Abby, would you mix the punch?"

"That's my job!" Millicent cried. "I'm supposed to make the punch." How could she be the chief helper if her mother took the important jobs away from her? But her mother left to finish setting the table.

Suddenly the small kitchen was very busy and very cramped. Mrs. Adams and Karen hustled back and forth, carrying platters and dishes. Abby poured bottles of cranberry juice and ginger ale into a big glass bowl.

Millicent stared at the array of spice jars arranged on a shelf over the stove. "What did she say to sprinkle?" she whispered to Roberta. She didn't want to have to ask her mother — the chief helper got orders right the first time.

"I don't remember," Roberta said. "Maybe this one." She reached for a jar labeled "Paprika."

"Abby," Millicent called. "What color is the stuff we're supposed to sprinkle on the salads?"

"Green." Abby floated an icy ring of frozen strawberries in the punch.

"That's not it," Millicent said to Roberta. "That stuff is red. Here, this must be it." She took a jar labeled "Oregano" off the shelf. "We have to use lots of it. Make it pretty." She dusted the pasta salads liberally with the dried herb. Then she and Roberta carried the bowls into the dining room.

The party was in full swing. All the chairs were occupied. Some of the younger guests were seated on cushions on the floor. Gaily wrapped gifts overflowed the bassinet. Millicent was glad her present, in its Santa Claus wrapping paper, stood out among the traditional teddy bear and baby duck wrappings.

Everyone good-naturedly teased Geneva about the coming arrival as they played the games in the baby bottle booklets that Millicent and Abby had put together.

But no one remarked on how cute Millicent was.

There was plenty of opportunity, as Millicent and Roberta took turns handing Geneva shower gifts to open. Roberta kept showing off, twirling as she presented each package to Geneva. One woman asked Roberta if she took lessons, and Roberta replied that she did, ice-skating lessons. She was clearly everyone's favorite.

Millicent tried to glide gracefully across the room in her ballet slippers so everyone would ask *her* if she took ballet lessons, even though she didn't. She tripped over the leg of the coffee table and nearly fell headlong into the lap of Lyman's mother. Mrs. Adams caught her arm just in time.

"Why don't you come help me? It'll soon be time to eat."

"I'm helping give this party," Millicent boasted loudly, snagging her foot in a tangle of ribbons that she dragged across the carpet until Karen bent down and freed her foot.

In the kitchen, Mrs. Adams ran a wet knife inside the salad molds.

"*I'm* supposed to do that," Millicent said.

"You're not getting anywhere near these salads," her mother declared. "Take those napkins out, please."

Millicent laid the napkins near a glass dish of yellow and white mints. She stuck her finger in the punch bowl and licked it. The punch tasted kind of weak. Obviously Abby hadn't made it right. If *she* had made the punch, it would be delicious.

Everything else looked so perfect — it was a shame to serve weak punch. Millicent glanced back into the kitchen. Mrs. Adams was maneuvering a wiggly salad onto a plate. Millicent wisely decided not to bother her. She saw a big bottle of lemon juice on the counter. That ought to add some tang to the punch. She emptied the entire bottle of juice into the punch bowl just before the guests trooped in.

After the grown-ups had filled their plates, the party-givers fixed their own plates. Millicent helped herself to fifteen ripe olives, but Mrs. Adams made her put thirteen back. She and Roberta squabbled over who would get the piece of cake with the yellow roses. Millicent wished her mother hadn't invited Roberta. The party would have been a lot more fun if she had been the only nine-year-old helper. Gingerly balancing plate and punch cup, Millicent went into the living room and sat down on the floor.

"This pasta has an . . . odd flavor," one woman remarked, inspecting a green-flecked forkful.

"So does the punch." Lyman's mother began coughing and had to be thumped on the back. "What's *in* it?" she wheezed.

Mrs. Adams hastily sipped her punch. "It tastes awful — like pure lemon juice. Abby, what did you do to it?"

"I didn't put lemon juice in the punch!" Abby denied. "Just ginger ale and cranberry juice, like the recipe."

Millicent sipped her own punch. Her mouth puckered. It *was* awful! How was she to know lemon juice would taste so terrible? She was only trying to make the punch better. She glanced guiltily at Abby, who was apologizing for the acidy punch. She ought to own up, not let her sister take the blame.

No one was eating their pasta salads. Millicent didn't like cold pasta, so she didn't put any on her plate.

Geneva put down her fork, making a face. "Mother, why did you add oregano to the pasta?"

"Oregano?" Mrs. Adams glanced suspiciously at Millicent. Then she laughed. "I think there were too many cooks in the kitchen today!"

The others laughed with her. As the party broke up, everyone declared that this had been the most interesting baby shower they'd ever been to.

Roberta twirled one last time for the parting company, making her skirt flare. Everyone clapped at her performance.

"Your helpers certainly added spice to the party," Lyman's mother said to Mrs. Adams. The women laughed heartily at the joke. Mrs. Adams confided that Millicent had accidently put her *shoes* in one of the molded salads. That sent Lyman's mother into peals of giggles.

Millicent wished she could miraculously make herself disappear. She wanted to be the cute chief helper, everyone's favorite. Not the one they *laughed* at.

Her mother would undoubtedly tell Mr. Adams about the party. Her father would shake his head sadly. "Millicent will never make it as favorite child. We might as well pick one of our other children."

Feeling sorry for herself, Millicent twirled. Her skirt belled out and her black ballet slippers flashed. She came to a stop without tripping or knocking anything over. It was a perfect twirl. But no one saw it.

# 7

When Millicent got home from the party, she walked up to Mrs. Taylor's house to give her a piece of stork cake.

Mrs. Taylor seemed happy to see her, as always. "Oh, you've brought me goodies! How nice."

"This is part of the stork's leg," Millicent said, in case Mrs. Taylor had trouble identifying what her piece of cake was supposed to be. "I also brought you this little basket with mints. They gave them out at the end. This one's mine, but I don't want it."

Mrs. Taylor admired the yellow basket with the tiny plastic stork tied to the handle with a ribbon. "A new baby coming. Isn't it wonderful?" Then she looked at Millicent. "Thank you, dear, but don't you want a souvenir of Geneva's shower to keep?"

Millicent shook her head mournfully. "I want to forget about the party, not remember it." She found herself telling Mrs. Taylor about the shoe in the salmon mousse, and the wrong green stuff on the pasta salads, and the too-lemony punch.

She even told her how Roberta had captured everyone's attention, stealing the limelight away from Millicent, her best friend.

"I don't know if I want to be her friend any more," she concluded. "It's hard being friends with somebody like Roberta. She's so little and cute. Everyone says so. All they ever say about me is I'm growing like a weed."

Mrs. Taylor smiled. A web of fine lines stretched across her cheeks. "Do I detect a note of jealousy?"

"I'm not jealous, really. But it's hard being friends with a girl who has green suede boots and can ski down the Bunny Slope." Millicent bent to pet a white long-haired cat who came over to sniff her shoes. Probably smelled like salmon mousse, she thought. "Roberta was the favorite at the party. I was — what's the oppposite of favorite? Unfavorite?"

"Out of favor," Mrs. Taylor supplied.

That was it exactly. She felt out of favor, which she imagined was closely related to being out of sorts. Not only that, she needed a new miracle to help get her father out of the dumps. He'd be even more depressed when he learned how Millicent nearly ruined Geneva's baby shower. How had so many problems piled up in such a short time? she wondered.

"Millicent," Mrs. Taylor said gently. "If it's any consolation, Roberta will probably remain petite all her life, but you will grow up tall and graceful, like a strong, young tree. I can tell."

"Can you really? When will this happen?" Millicent couldn't wait to lord it over Roberta that she was going to be tall and strong like a tree when she grew up.

"Not for quite a while, I'm afraid. You'll have to endure being the tallest in your class for a few more years. But it'll pay off, I promise."

Her heart sank again. She wouldn't be tall and graceful for years! Why was it all the good things were always years off in the future? If only Mrs. Taylor had said, "Tomorrow, Millicent. Tomorrow you'll wake up and be tall and graceful."

It was getting late. Millicent put her coat back on and told Mrs. Taylor good-bye. At home, she opened the front door cautiously, worried she was still out of favor.

Rudy bounded across the living room. "Guess what?" he said. "Mom's coming to school."

"What for?" Millicent was instantly alert. Had Mrs. Stann called her mother in for a meeting? She hadn't done anything wrong lately, except the time Bruce got her in trouble for talking in class and that was all *his* fault.

Mrs. Adams answered the question herself. "I'm meeting with the surveyors Monday morning. If this clear weather holds, they said they'd be able to survey the playground tomorrow."

"What's a surveyor?" Rudy asked.

"It's someone who measures land. He'll mark the boundaries of the playground. We need lots of room for the new playground equipment."

Millicent had been wondering about something. "Why do we need a new playground? There's nothing wrong with our old one."

"The equipment is old," Mrs. Adams explained. "The teeter-totter is so rusty, the little kids can barely make it teeter." Millicent giggled. "Mainly, we want to move the playground. The Maple Hills development comes right up to the school boundary. It's not a good idea to have children playing next to houses. We're moving your playground around to the side, where there is more open space. And we're going to build some terrific new equipment."

"Swings and slides?"

"That and more. A climber, a jungle gym, and a primary unit for the little kids." Mrs. Adams glanced at the clock. "I want to call Geneva. I hope she's putting her feet up like the doctor ordered. It was a big day for her."

It had been a big day for Millicent, too, but not the kind of day she wanted people to remember.

On Monday, Millicent and Rudy rode to school with their mother, instead of walking. Millicent escorted her mother to the main office. Mrs. Adams looked very pretty in her purple suit and white blouse with the floppy tie. She called it her "president of the PTA" outfit.

Millicent pointed out her essay and drawing on the bulletin board by the office. "That's mine," she said proudly.

Mrs. Adams paused to read Millicent's essay. "You wrote about a tree! How refreshing. And it's very well written, too. When Mrs. Stann gives you back your paper, I'd like to put it on the refrigerator at home."

Rudy banged his GI Joe lunchbox against one leg. "I'll draw you a picture, Mom. And you can put it on the refrigerator."

"You do that, Rudy. Well, guys, better scoot to class. I'll see you this afternoon." She blew them a kiss.

As Millicent turned to head down the hall, she saw Roberta enter the building with Craig and Sheila Sanders.

"Hi," Roberta said, as if nothing had happened Saturday. "Your Mom drove you?"

"She has a meeting. You walked with Craig and Sheila?"

Roberta wrinkled her nose. "It wasn't my idea, believe me. Sheila whined the whole way, and Craig kept kicking this rock at my feet. I finally had to punch him. I don't know how your brother stands him."

"Rudy likes everybody," Millicent said. He was such a nice kid. She wondered if he would feel bad when she became the family favorite. Then she noticed that Roberta was wearing ordinary shoes today. No fancy green suede boots. She guessed she would stay friends with Roberta. It really wasn't Roberta's fault she was little and cute and everyone liked her best.

Together, they walked to Room 6. Bruce was in his seat. He tipped his desk back on two legs so he could talk to Millicent.

"I saw your mom in the office. Are you in trouble again, Millie? Or is she coming back to school?"

"No, silly. She's here on *business*. My mom is head of the playground committee. She's getting us a new playground."

"I like the old playground."

"Well, we're getting a new one." Who cared what Bruce Johnston liked?

"Millicent," Mrs. Stann said. "Would you and Bruce like to join us? Bruce, four legs on the floor." The other kids snickered. Millicent's cheeks grew hot. Darn that Bruce!

They had an activity sheet first, math problems using Roman numerals instead of regular numbers. It was hard work. Millicent kept mixing up XI and IX. She was glad the Roman number system hadn't lasted. Real numbers were easier to write.

Suddenly Bruce yelled loud enough to be heard in Rome, "Some guy is spying on us!"

Everyone looked out the window. Sure enough, a man crouched outside their window. He wasn't spying on them, though. He was hunched over a peculiar instrument that reminded Millicent of a telescope, squinting through the eyepiece. Another man stood several yards away, holding a long pole upright.

"I know who they are," Millicent spoke up.

"Surveyors. They're marking our new playground."

"Millicent's right," Mrs. Stann said. "Those men are surveying the new playground. We wouldn't want part of our playground on someone else's property. That's all the excitement, class. Let's get busy."

They worked on Roman numerals until the bell rang for recess. As Millicent filed outside with the others, Bruce stuck his foot out. She stumbled into the water fountain.

"Have a nice trip," he teased. "See you in the fall."

Millicent rubbed her hip where she'd bumped into the hard porcelain fixture. "I wish he'd transfer to another school," she grumbled to Roberta.

"He likes you," Roberta declared simply.

"Likes me! All he does is bug me."

Roberta skipped down the steps to the blacktop. "Bruce just wants you to notice him. That's a boy's way of showing a girl he likes her."

"By half-killing her?" Millicent checked the playground. "Where is he, anyway? I want to stay far away from him." The boys were playing kickball in the grassy field that bordered the new houses of Maple Hills.

"Let's go sit on the swings," Roberta suggested.

Sitting on the swings did not appeal to Millicent. The swings were so old the seats were splintery, even though they were sanded and repainted every spring. By this spring, though, they would have brand-new swings. Maybe with padded seats.

"I want to visit my tree," Millicent said. "I haven't said hello to it lately."

"You say hello to trees?" Roberta giggled, running to keep up with Millicent.

"This tree I do. It's my special place, remember?"

She was glad the big maple tree was her special place. She could visit it any time she wanted. Roberta could only go to her special place, Disney World, on a plane, and Bruce could only go to Wild World in the summertime, when the park was open. They hadn't picked very convenient special places, in Millicent's opinion.

The side part of the schoolyard was the prettiest, Millicent thought, even though the front had flowering shrubs by the wide steps that led to the main office. On this side there were lots of trees and bushes that grew by themselves. Birds hopped back and forth in the branches of Millicent's tree. They liked her tree, too. Millicent saw stakes driven into the ground, with colored ribbons tied to them. Different-colored ribbons had been tied to some of the bushes.

Roberta stared at a white van parked along the curb. "The surveyor men are still here."

One man was loading the telescope or whatever it was into the van. The other man saw them and waved. The girls waved back.

"Oh, no!" Millicent cried. "Look who's coming!"

Bruce Johnston and Lorenzo Scrementi raced across the field, yelling like pirates. Bruce held a folded paper cupped over one hand. A Cootie Catcher!

Shrieking, Millicent ducked behind the thick, sheltering trunk of the maple tree. Bruce chased her around and around the tree. He grabbed a strand of her hair with his Cootie Catcher.

"Got one!" he cried triumphantly. He made a dramatic show of squashing the "cootie."

"Go away, Bruce!" Millicent shouted.

"Not until I've done my duty and killed all the cooties in Room 6." He sprang forward, this time clutching her arm in the Cootie Catcher.

Millicent jerked her arm free. "I mean it, Bruce. I'm telling Mrs. Stann if you don't leave me alone."

Lorenzo was obviously tired of the game. "Come on," he urged Bruce. "I don't want to stay after school again today." Whenever Bruce got in trouble, which was almost daily, Mrs. Stann made him stay late. Because Lorenzo was always with Bruce, he got in trouble, too, and shared the punishment.

Bruce saluted with his Cootie Catcher. "Just call me the Cootie Man, at your service."

"I'm going to call the teacher if you don't get out of here," Millicent said angrily. She couldn't even enjoy a peaceful five minutes at her special place without Bruce bothering her.

The boys sauntered over to talk to the surveyors.

"*Boys!*" Millicent remarked with disgust. "Why do we have to have them, anyway?"

"Who knows?" Roberta shrugged. "My father says most of the world's problems are caused by poor planning. Like traffic and pollution and stuff. Maybe the reason we have boys is because of poor planning."

"Well, they aren't in *my* plan," Millicent said emphatically. She remembered then that she needed to think of a new miracle. Maybe two miracles. One to make her father feel better, and one to get rid of Bruce Johnston.

"Uh-oh," Roberta said. "Guess who's coming back."

Millicent picked a stick off the ground. "If Bruce starts that cootie business again, I'm going to let him have it."

But the boys were full of information about the surveyors' job. Bruce declared he was going to be a surveyor when he grew up.

"See those trees with orange ribbons?" he said. "Those are the ones that are going to be cut down. And those green ribbons on the stakes mark the edges of our playground."

"Why are they cutting down the trees?" Roberta wanted to know.

Lorenzo answered, "That's where the playground equipment is supposed to go."

Millicent knew all about the new playground equipment. "We're getting a jungle gym and a thing called a climber. The little kids are getting a fancy primary unit. Better than the old stuff." She leaned dreamily against the maple trunk. "I can stay at my special place every day during recess. My tree will be in the middle of the new playground."

"What special place?" Bruce asked.

"Here." She patted the trunk. "This is my special place. Didn't you read my essay on the bulletin board by the office?"

"Nah. I never read that junk."

"Well, you should. Maybe you'd learn something. Then you'd know how much I love this tree. It's a lot better than Wild World," she added smugly. "A lot closer, too."

Bruce narrowed his eyes at a spot just above Millicent's head. "I wouldn't love this tree too much if I were you, Millie."

"Don't call me Millie. Why not?"

"Look up there."

Millicent looked up. An orange ribbon circled a stout branch. The ends fluttered loosely in the breeze, but the ribbon had been tied quite deliberately. It wouldn't blow away.

She knew immediately what the orange ribbon meant.

The maple tree was going to be cut down. Her tree was doomed.

# 8

After school, Millicent went straight home. Roberta asked her if she wanted to come over and play. Ordinarily Millicent loved to play at Roberta's house, but she shook her head.

"I have to ask Mom about my tree," she said. "If it's true."

"Maybe Bruce was wrong," Roberta said consolingly. She knew how upset Millicent was. It was a terrible thing, learning that your special place was about to be cut down. Suppose someone came along and tied a big orange ribbon around Disney World? Not that anyone *would*, but the idea was the same.

"Mo-om!" Millicent cried anxiously before she was barely in the front door.

"We're in here," Mrs. Adams called from the kitchen.

Millicent threw her knapsack on the sofa and ran out to the kitchen. Her mother was not alone.

Geneva sat at the table, drinking a glass of milk. Rudy hung on the back of her chair, touching her now and then as if making sure she was real. It had been a long time since he had seen Geneva. She didn't come over to their house very often.

"Surprise!" her sister sang out. "Bet you didn't expect to see me."

Millicent hurried over to give her big sister a hug. "How did you get here? Your car's not out front."

"I brought her home with me," Mrs. Adams replied. "We worked on the nursery this afternoon. I put up wallpaper." The nursery was the baby's bedroom. All the presents Geneva received at her shower would go into this special room.

"And then we went shopping," Geneva went on. "I decided to come home with Mom and have supper here. Mom's fixing my favorite — fried chicken and mashed potatoes."

It had been a long time since her mother had made Millicent's favorite, chipped beef with gravy over biscuits. Was there any point trying to be the favorite child? she wondered. It seemed Geneva had already been chosen.

"Which reminds me," Mrs. Adams said, pushing herself away from the table. "I'd better start supper."

"Let me help," Geneva offered. "I can still peel potatoes." The closer Geneva got to having her baby, the less she felt like doing, she admitted. Standing, walking, even driving, made her tired.

"How will you get home?" Millicent asked her sister.

"Lyman will pick me up later this evening."

Millicent's brother-in-law taught at a private school in Virginia, not too far from where the Adamses lived. He was still taking classes at the University of Maryland for his master's degree. Geneva had been taking classes, too, but she'd stopped until after the baby was born.

Then Millicent remembered she had something important to ask her mother.

"Mom, those surveyor men came to our school today — " she began.

"Yes, I know. I met them. They were able to survey the entire playground. Weren't we lucky to schedule them before the weather turned bad? It's going to rain tomorrow."

"Better rain than snow," Geneva commented. "I can't believe we haven't had any snow yet this year. I'm worried about next month. It *always* snows in February."

"I wish we'd have a gizzard!" Rudy exclaimed.

Mrs. Adams and Geneva burst out laughing. "Blizzard, not gizzard," Geneva said. "And please don't wish for a blizzard, Rudy."

Mrs. Adams patted Geneva's shoulder. "Don't worry, sweetie. It won't snow when you have to go to the hospital."

"You know that tree?" Millicent interrupted loudly, trying to steer the conversation away from babies and blizzards back to her maple tree. "The one next to my room? Those men put an orange ribbon around it. Bruce Johnston said it's to mark the trees that'll be cut down. Is that true?"

Her mother handed a sack of potatoes and the peeler to Geneva. “Yes, the surveyors were supposed to tag trees and bushes that are going to be cut down. We have to make room for the new equipment.”

“But, Mom,” Millicent protested. “My *favorite tree* is one of the ones going to be cut down. You know, the one I wrote about in my essay? My special place?”

Mrs. Adams stopped flouring the chicken to stare at her. “Oh, Millicent. The big maple tree. I didn’t realize it was *that* tree. I’m awfully sorry, honey.”

“Mom, you can’t let them cut it down. Can we take the ribbon off?”

Her mother shook her head regretfully. “It has to come down, Millicent. That’s where we’re putting the climber. You’ll like the climber. It’s like a treehouse, with steps and platforms. That could be your new special place,” she suggested.

“Not mine,” Millicent said morosely. “Everybody in the school will use the climber. The maple tree was my very own special place. And now you’re cutting it down.”

“I’m sorry, dear,” Mrs. Adams said kindly. “I wish I could change the plans, but I can’t. It took the committee longer than I thought to approve the plans. We can’t afford to waste any more time — we have to complete the new playground by spring and we have a lot of work to do before then.”

Millicent wasn't about to give up so easily. "It's just one tree. What can one tree hurt?"

"The tree doesn't *hurt* anything," her mother replied. "We need that location for the climber. The climber and the primary unit are the biggest pieces of playground equipment. We need lots of room for them."

"We don't want a climber," Millicent declared. "Leave the tree instead."

Her mother came over to collect the bowl of potatoes Geneva had peeled and diced. "Millicent, it's not up to me to make that decision. Or you. The committee and the PTA worked for weeks planning your new playground. Your tree will be cut down for the good of many, many children."

"It sure won't be for the good of the tree."

Then Abby came home. As soon as she saw Geneva, she squealed as if they hadn't seen each other for years. It was always that way with the two older sisters. They didn't mean to ignore the "little kids," as they called Millicent and Rudy, but they did.

"I didn't get a chance to ask you Saturday," Geneva said to Abby. "How is school?"

Abby sighed. "I haven't started my big anthropology paper yet. I'll have to get cracking this weekend."

"The one about the scientist from the future?" Geneva asked.

"Yeah, I have to pretend I've never seen this house before and try to figure out who once lived here." She glanced around the kitchen with a frown. "It won't be very interesting, though. We have such an ordinary house."

"We're ordinary people," Mrs. Adams put in.

"I was thinking," Abby said, "of asking Mrs. Taylor if I could use her house instead. All those Hollywood mementos she has lying around . . . it would be so neat to write about."

Mrs. Adams gave Abby a look. "But that wouldn't be very honest, would it?"

"No," Abby said resignedly. "I'll have to use our house, ordinary as it is."

Millicent felt left out. Her mother was busy with supper, and her sisters were chattering a mile a minute.

Nobody cared that her favorite tree in the world was going to fall under the ax. Her mother thought the climber would be just as good. How could a dumb wooden platform take the place of a real live tree? Would the climber provide shade in the summer? Did leaves grow on it? Would she be able to dream under the climber the way she dreamed sitting under her tree?

The phone rang. Mrs. Adams answered it. The call must have been about the new playground because Mrs. Adams asked the person on the other end to hold while she got her folder. "I'm taking this on the extension," she told Abby. "Hang up the kitchen phone, please."

"Mom's really busy," Geneva observed. Then she noticed Millicent disconsolately chewing her thumbnail. "What's the matter, bug?" Her sister used to call Millicent "bug" when she was little.

"I'm out of sorts," Millicent replied.

"Over what?"

"You heard Mom. They're cutting my *tree* down. It's my favorite tree, and it's being chopped down."

"So do something about it," Geneva said matter-of-factly.

"Like what?" She couldn't even think of a new miracle to help her father, much less save a tree.

"Protest. You know, have a demonstration to protest chopping the tree down."

Millicent had no idea what her sister was talking about. "I don't know what you mean."

Abby hung up the phone and joined the discussion. "When you don't like something, you protest against it. People are always marching in Washington against the arms race and stuff like that. You've seen them on TV, carrying big signs on Capitol Hill or around the White House."

"Back in the sixties, protesting was very popular," Geneva said. "College kids used to have these sit-ins. They'd sit down and they wouldn't get up until they made their point. Mom used to protest a lot."

"Mom did sit-ins?" Millicent said incredulously. She pictured her mother sitting in a rocking chair on the White House lawn.

"She sure did. Mom used to be involved in a lot of causes. Dad told me she was forever circulating petitions."

"Petitions? What are they?" Millicent asked, astonished to discover this new side of her mother.

Abby explained. "You go around and collect signatures, get people to agree to your cause. A whole lot of signatures can sometimes change a law, or the way people think."

"Maybe you can get the kids at school to organize a rally," Geneva said. "Or stage a demonstration yourself. Even one voice speaking out is better than complete silence."

Sit-ins, rallies, petitions. Her sisters' suggestions whirled in Millicent's head like leaves in the wind.

"Go for it, Millicent," Abby urged. "What have you got to lose?"

Confused, Millicent went to her room to think. She stretched across her bed, pulling Jocko off her pillow.

"What should I do?" she asked her stuffed monkey.

Her mother had said the plans for the playground couldn't be changed. They couldn't simply untie the orange ribbon and leave the maple tree where it was.

Millicent felt sorry for the big maple tree. Nobody except her wanted it. The maple tree was out of favor, just as she was. She knew exactly how it felt to be the opposite of favorite. It was a terrible feeling, whether you were a girl or a tree.

"I think the tree ought to have a chance," she said to Jocko.

But she wasn't sure how to go about organizing a protest. She could ask her mother, who was apparently an old hand at protesting, but Mrs. Adams was the person Millicent wanted to protest *against*. Well, not against her mother, but what her mother was *doing*. After all, her mother drew up the plans that called for chopping the maple tree down in the first place. Maybe it wouldn't be so difficult, staging a protest. She'd start small.

"I'm going to go for it," Millicent said firmly.

Her stuffed monkey said nothing, but his black shoe-button eyes seem to agree with her decision.

The next morning a freezing rain slanted against the windowpanes. On cold rainy days Mrs. Adams drove Millicent and Rudy to school.

Millicent dressed hurriedly, then went out to the kitchen. Rudy had already eaten. Crumbs from his toast were all over the counter. Pouring herself a bowl of cereal, she sat in her usual place at the table. She ate quickly, glancing at the clock.

Nobody knew it yet, but Millicent was staging a sit-in. A one-person sit-in. She was going to sit there and not get up again until her mother promised to change the plans.

At a quarter to nine, Mrs. Adams came in and scooped her keyring from the basket on the kitchen counter. Millicent folded her arms and tried to look determined. Her private demonstration had officially begun.

"OK," Mrs. Adams said to her. "Rinse your

bowl and get your coat on. Rudy! Time to leave!" She disappeared into the laundry room.

Millicent remained in her chair.

Rudy skipped in, wearing his rain slicker. "I'm ready, Mom."

Mrs. Adams returned, fumbling with a bent umbrella. "Abby has about fourteen umbrellas in her car. I wish she'd remember there are other people in the family who might not want to get wet. . . . Millicent, I told you to get moving. You're going to be late. Now come on."

Millicent didn't budge.

"Did you hear me, young lady?" Her mother was starting to lose patience. "Get out of that chair."

"I can't," Millicent stated. "I'm doing a sit-in."

Her mother's eyebrows rose. "A *what*?"

"A sit-in. You know, like you used to do back in the olden days." She locked her feet around the rungs of the chair.

A wry smile played at the corners of her mother's mouth. "Oh, yes. Back when I joined in the Boston Tea Party. Millicent, I don't know what it is you are sitting-in *for*, but you're going to school, regardless."

Now what was she going to do? She had to go to school — her father once told her it was the law. But she couldn't break her sit-in. Geneva said protesters didn't give up until they made their point.

But she didn't have to have a *chair* to do her

sit-in. If she just stayed in a sitting position, that ought to count. Easing herself away from the kitchen table, Millicent hobbled over to retrieve her knapsack.

Her mother watched her crab across the room. "What's the matter with your back?"

"Nothing," Millicent replied. "I'm doing my sit-in, only without the chair. You can tell, can't you?"

Mrs. Adams helped Millicent into her rain jacket. "You look like your father did the time he fell off the stepladder. Millicent, *why* are you 'doing a sit-in,' as you say."

"To save my tree. When you change the plans, I'll walk right."

"I bet you've been listening to Geneva," Mrs. Adams said. "Millicent, you can't walk around like that all *day*."

"Yes, I can." Actually, she wasn't so sure she *could* stay bent over the whole day. Her back hurt already.

Sheila and Craig Sanders ran into the kitchen. They were riding with them to school. Roberta would have gone with them, too, but she had the sniffles and Mrs. Holloway was keeping her home.

Sheila stared at Millicent. "What's the matter with you?"

"Millicent's doing a sit-in!" Rudy said as they splashed out to the car.

Millicent shuffled out behind them. In her stooped position, she couldn't see anything but the ground. At least she could sit in the car.

At school, she had a little trouble getting out of the car. Rudy led her up the steps. Kids gawked at her as she lurched into the building. Millicent was horribly embarrassed, but she had to let her mother see that she wasn't quitting just because she had to go out in public. School or no school, her protest went on.

As she scuttled past the main office, a familiar voice called her name.

"Hey, Millie!" Bruce elephant-walked beside her, imitating her posture. "What's the matter? You got arthur-itis?"

"For your information, I'm doing a sit-in. To save my maple tree. But I had to come to school, so I'm doing my sit-in without a chair. Do you mind?"

"I don't mind. I just think you look weird."

"I don't care what you think," she said with as much grandeur as she could summon doubled over.

Millicent was glad when she reached her classroom. "Good morning, Mrs. Stann," she said, hobbling past her teacher's desk.

"Millicent!" Mrs. Stann cried in alarm. "Did you have an accident?"

"She's doing a sit-in," Bruce answered for her. "To save a dumb old tree."

"I see," Mrs. Stann said weakly, but Millicent didn't think her teacher saw at all.

Millicent tried to stick to her sit-in the whole day, but it often wasn't convenient and she kept forgetting. Bruce reminded her, even pushing her head down a couple of times. Her back ached, but at least she was getting her point across.

Teachers and other students stopped her several times to ask what was wrong. Millicent used the opportunity to tell them about the doomed tree. Several kids agreed it was too nice a tree to be chopped down.

When the last bell rang, Millicent trudged down the hall, upright. She was tired of walking bent over like an old lady.

"Guess what, Millie?" Bruce Johnston pointed at the bulletin board. "They took your essay down. Look what's up there now."

Millicent checked the bulletin board.

Sure enough, the "Special Place" compositions had been removed. A huge color drawing covered the entire bulletin board. The picture showed what the new playground would look like when it was finished, with the fort and the jungle gym and the other equipment. The climber, a wooden structure with platforms and stairs, stood where the maple tree had once been.

Looking at the drawing, Millicent felt sad. It was as if the maple tree had never existed. Her sit-in, brief as it was, had been for nothing.

"Tough luck, Millie," Bruce said. "Looks like your tree is history!"

# 9

Millicent breathed a steamy circle on the chilly picture window. Before the vapor faded, she drew a tree. Resting her face against the glass, she thought about how dreary her life was, and on a Saturday, too.

According to her calculations, she had struck out three times in only a few weeks. First with the newspaper, which was a flop because no one subscribed. Second, the disastrous miracle she performed for her father. And last, the sit-in for her maple tree.

If she wanted to be a hundred percent accurate, she could include the times she had fallen out of favor with her parents, when she had wrecked her father's study, messed up her mother's blueprints, and nearly ruined Geneva's baby shower.

It looked as if her tree would fall under the ax, the city dump would remain her father's permanent address, and she, Millicent Teresa Adams, might as well find a new family to be the favorite in. On Mars.

Mrs. Adams came into the living room, carrying

her briefcase and coat. "Your father is making lunch, Millicent. If you go outside, bundle up."

It had turned very cold overnight. The sky was so clear it was as if the world were encased in a glass dome. Millicent couldn't believe it was already February and not one flake of snow had fallen yet. Rudy would probably never get to use his new snow saucer. They both longed for a no-school snow day. Millicent wanted to hear her mother come into her room and tell her not to get out of bed, the radio announcer said school was cancelled, to look out the window and see great sheets of snow falling gently on their yard, making familiar objects into strange new shapes.

Her mother slid file folders into her briefcase. "Well, I'm off to school. My meeting is in ten minutes."

"Are you going to ask them about keeping my tree?" Millicent said.

Mrs. Adams touched her cheek briefly. "Your face is cold. Honey, the landscaping plan is all set. We've got bigger problems to worry about now. Like how we're going to raise money for the seventy-five tons of pea gravel we need for the base of the primary unit."

What was more important? Saving a tree or buying a bunch of gravel? As far as Millicent was concerned, there was no comparison.

The house echoed with Saturday afternoon stillness. Millicent didn't have anything to do. Roberta was at her skating lesson. Abby was doing homework in her room.

She found her father making sandwiches in the kitchen. Rudy licked peanut butter off a knife.

He held out the gummy knife. "Want some?"

"No, thanks." She leaned on the counter, watching her father work. "Daddy, did we ever have a winter without snow before?"

"I don't think so." He screwed the lid on the peanut butter jar. "It'll snow, don't worry. Winter isn't over yet."

"We haven't had a no-school snow day this whole year," Millicent complained. "Did you ever have to stay home from school because of snow?"

"Are you kidding? When I was in fourth grade, I had to battle six-foot snow drifts — on foot!"

"Were you ever in fourth grade?" Rudy asked his father incredulously.

Millicent gave him a scornful look. "Don't be silly. Of course Daddy was in the fourth grade. How do you think he got to the fifth grade?"

They had finished their sandwiches when Abby walked in.

"Dad," she said pleadingly. "Will you do me a big, *big* favor?"

"What?" he asked. Mr. Adams was the only person Millicent knew who answered that question with "What?" instead of "Depends on what it is." He always seemed willing to do anything for his children. Well, almost anything.

"I'd like the house to myself for a while to work

on my anthropology report," Abby said. "About an hour."

"We won't make any noise," Mr. Adams said. "The place is as quiet as a tomb now."

"No, see, I have to be here *alone*." She waved her hands, as if to make them all vanish. "I want to rearrange some of our family's belongings — not too many, just a few — to make our house more interesting. If I were an archeologist from the future, I'd die of boredom trying to analyze our house."

Mr. Adams sighed. "That report . . . Abby, exactly what do you want to do to the house? Paint the walls black?"

"No, just move things around a little."

"You're not touching Jocko!" Millicent cried.

"And you can't touch my Matchbox cars," Rudy chimed.

"I won't bother your toys." Abby looked at Mr. Adams. "Well, Dad?"

He seemed reluctant. "I don't think you ought to move the furniture. . . ."

"Oh, I won't move any of the furniture. I just want to put some things around to make the place more . . . colorful. Please, Daddy. Take the little kids out for a while. To the mall or something."

"Yeah!" Millicent agreed eagerly, not even minding being called a little kid. "Take me and Rudy to Fair Oaks."

Mr. Adams rubbed his forehead. "I am not going to wade through the Saturday crowds at

Fair Oaks. We'll take a walk." To Abby, he added a warning, "Don't mess up the house too much."

"I won't," Abby promised cheerfully. "I'm just going to sprinkle a few good relics around for my imaginary archeologist to discover."

Mr. Adams took his old jacket off the hook in the laundry room. "Your imaginary archeologist could discover me. I feel like a relic myself these days."

Millicent wasn't too disappointed they weren't going to the mall. At least she'd be with her father. They could be down in the dumps together.

The three of them ambled down Wagner Avenue.

"The Scheinberg place is still vacant, I see," Mr. Adams remarked, gazing thoughtfully at the neat brick house at the end of the street. "I don't know what it is about that house, but it doesn't stay occupied very long."

"Maybe it's haunted," Millicent said.

Rudy went "Oooooooh," like a ghost.

"I guess it's too close to the barricade," Mr. Adams said. "People are afraid the street will be finished someday and they'll catch a lot of traffic going into Maple Hills."

"Are they going to finish our street?" Millicent wondered.

"Who knows? Besides, I like it unfinished."

Millicent was surprised to hear her father admit this. She liked living on an unfinished street, but she had believed she was the only one who did.

To her, the possibilities were limitless. When — and if — the road builder came back, their street could go anywhere.

They edged around the concrete barrier and cut across the field to Maple Hills. Soon they had walked as far as Green Acres Elementary.

Millicent pointed to Mrs. Adams' car. "Mom's having a meeting in there. She's worried about pea gravel."

"This playground project is turning out to be bigger than your mother originally thought," Mr. Adams acknowledged.

Rudy yanked at his father's arm. "Daddy, I want to show you my windows. Our class made snowflakes. I want to show you mine."

They dutifully trooped around the side of the building to the windows of Rudy's second-grade class. Mr. Adams praised Rudy's snowflake, which looked like a scrap of torn paper to Millicent.

"Probably the only snowflakes we'll see this year," she commented.

Then they went to Millicent's classroom, on the other side of the building.

"We don't have any pictures on the windows, but you can look in at my desk," Millicent said. They cupped their hands against the glass and looked in Mrs. Stann's room. Millicent had left in such a hurry Friday afternoon, she forgot to straighten the papers sticking out of the cubby under her seat. She was a little embarrassed for her father to see how untidy she was, but he didn't say anything.

He stood under the sheltering branches of the maple tree, shoving his hands deep in his pockets.

Millicent patted the trunk. "That's my tree."

"Oh? I didn't see your name on it," Mr. Adams said, smiling.

"Well, I don't really own it. But I like it a lot. I wrote about it as my special place." Her tone became crestfallen. "It won't be anybody's special place soon."

"Why?"

Millicent scraped at the bark with her fingernail. "Because it's going to be cut down. For the new playground. A whole bunch of trees and bushes are going to be chopped down."

Mr. Adams tipped his head back to take in the towering height of the maple tree. "This is far and away the nicest tree in the entire playground. I can't believe they're cutting it down."

"I wish they'd leave it." Millicent wrapped her arms around the trunk. "This tree is my friend."

Rudy copied, even though his spindly arms wouldn't reach all the way around. "This tree is my best friend in the world."

She frowned at him. "You don't even play up here. The little kids play down the hill."

"It's still my favorite tree!" Rudy insisted.

"It can't be *your* favorite tree — it's mine!"

Mr. Adams said, "Here comes your mother, kids. Break it up."

Sure enough, the double doors opened and people spilled down the steps. Mrs. Adams' committee meeting was over. She lingered on the steps, talking to a man in a felt hat and a trenchcoat. Millicent thought the man looked cold. He should have had on a down jacket, like her father. When they finished talking, Mrs. Adams rushed over to join them. Her face was flushed with triumph.

"Hi, everybody! Do you know who that was?"

"The President of the United States?" Rudy guessed.

Mrs. Adams laughed. "Almost. That was Mr. Murphy, the developer of Maple Hills! He donated five thousand dollars to our playground project. That'll pay for the primary unit and the jungle gym. And he suggested a way to pay for the seventy-five tons of pea gravel we need. We're going to have a Gravel Drive! Isn't that cute? We'll ask the parents to buy a ton of gravel for fifteen dollars and donate it in their child's name. To make it more personal, each child will receive a scoop of their very own pea gravel to use in their driveway at home."

Mr. Adams nodded. "It should work."

"Will you buy a ton of gravel for me and Rudy?" Millicent wanted to know. She planned to keep her scoop of gravel in a carton, to use as a pretend sandbox for Jocko.

"Of course. I'll be the first to sign you two up," Mrs. Adams said. "Thank heaven that headache is solved."

Mr. Adams rested his hand on the trunk of the maple tree. "Millicent tells me this tree is going to be cut down."

"Yes, it is. We're putting the climber there. The primary unit is the biggest piece — it has double slides, a tic-tac-toe board, and a C-shaped challenge ladder. It'll go over there. The jungle gym will go on the other side and the climber will be here."

"You're cutting down this magnificent tree for a thing called a climber?" Mr. Adams pressed. "You're cutting down a natural climber to put up an artificial one?"

"Paul, you know very well the children can't climb trees. The climber is safer. And this is the only place left to put it," Mrs. Adams said defensively.

"It just seems a shame to cut down the nicest tree in the schoolyard," Mr. Adams went on. "Look how big it is. It must be fifty years old. Think of all the history this tree has seen." In his enthusiasm, he ran his fingers through his hair, making the fine fringe around his bald spot stand up. "Why, this tree was a seedling during the Depression. A sapling during World War Two. . . ."

"I worked days with the committee to come up with a workable plan. I'd love to save this tree," Mrs. Adams admitted with an aggrieved sigh. "But it has to go. For the good of the children who need a safe place to play."

"I know," Mr. Adams said. "It's just a shame

that a tree that has lived so long has to be cut down."

Millicent watched her father with round eyes, astonished to see he wasn't mopey any more. He actually seemed interested in something, her tree! Maybe he was finally out of the dumps.

They all rode home with Mrs. Adams. When Mr. Adams opened the front door, he let out a yelp. "I think I'm in the wrong house."

"Doesn't it look neat?" Abby said.

She had completely rearranged the living room. Mrs. Adams' plants were clustered in front of the television set, blocking the screen in a leafy shield. The shoes of everyone in the family had been heaped on the couch.

"What on earth — ?" Mr. Adams picked his old tennis shoe off the end table.

"Don't touch that!" Abby cried. "I haven't finished yet."

"Don't tell me — Abby's anthropology report." Mrs. Adams plucked her blow dryer out of a vase. "I suppose she wants her imaginary archeologist to think we were weird people."

Mr. Adams headed for his study. Millicent followed, anxious to see what else Abby had done.

At first she didn't notice anything. The room looked the same as always. Then her father began taking books from the shelves.

"Abby!" he called. When she came to the doorway, he demanded, "Where are my history books? Where did all these best-sellers come from?"

"The library," Abby replied blithely. "I thought your books were too stuffy so I replaced them with best-sellers. The books are a clue to what decade we live in — it's a lot more clever than putting magazines or newspapers on the coffee table, don't you think?"

Mr. Adams had located a pile of history books behind his armchair. "Why does everyone feel the need to rearrange my books?" he muttered. "I object to having your professor think I only read mediocre novels, even if he *is* still wet behind the ears."

"Oh, Daddy," Abby sighed. "You're impossible these days."

Millicent silently agreed with her sister. If anything, her father was getting worse. Something must be done, and fast.

He had come to life briefly when they were discussing the fate of Millicent's maple tree. He didn't want it cut down any more than she did. Maybe there was one last miracle she could perform, she thought, as the idea slowly formed.

Suppose she waged an all-out campaign to save her tree, not just a puny sit-in? Her father would be convinced once and for all that one person could still make a difference.

She'd save the tree *and* her father at the same time.

# 10

As the third bus unloaded by the front door, Millicent raised her sign higher.

"Save the tree! Save the tree," she chanted, in case some of the kids couldn't read her sign.

A few kids looked over at her and pointed. Some laughed. But mainly they went inside the school, without giving Millicent more than a curious glance.

Millicent lowered her sign, frowning. So far, the students had largely ignored her. Geneva didn't tell her about *that* part.

The night before Millicent had called her sister in Maryland to ask for advice on staging a demonstration. Geneva advised her to carry a sign and chant a slogan. Protest demonstrations don't usually start so small, her sister had said. But as people realized what Millicent was fighting for, they would flock to her cause. Some protest marches end up on the evening news, or at the very least, a picture on the front page of the *Washington Post*. At the rate Millicent's demonstration was going, she couldn't even hope for a mention in the *Wagner Avenue Chronicle.*

It was almost nine o'clock. The buses were arriving one behind the other. And a huge group of walkers from Maple Hills came down the sidewalk.

As the first students stepped off the buses, Millicent held her sign up again and shouted, "Save the tree! Don't let them cut it down! Save the tree!"

"I think you're out of *your* tree!" a sixth-grade boy called.

Another big boy yelled, "Hey, look at the nutty squirrel! Somebody let her out of her cage."

Hecklers. Geneva had cautioned Millicent about them. Even the President had to put up with hecklers, people who yelled smart remarks. "Don't lose your cool," Geneva instructed. "If you let them see you're rattled by what they say, then nobody will believe in your cause."

"Who cares about a dumb old tree?" Sheila Sanders sneered as she walked by.

"You should!" Millicent cried. "We all should care! This is *our* tree and they're going to cut it down. It's the nicest tree for *miles* and we have to save it —"

"Save your breath," jeered a sixth-grade girl.

Millicent watched the older students stream into the school. The big kids were really giving her a hard time. She didn't understand it. They should be concerned about the maple tree. It was their school, too.

"If you're trying to get those guys interested, forget it."

Millicent spun around to see Bruce Johnston coming up the walk. "What do you mean, forget it?"

He waved toward the big kids bunched around the front door. "They're going to junior high next year. They could care less about what happens in this school."

"Well, they *should.*" Maybe Bruce had a point. She ought to target her cause toward the kids who were going to stay at Green Acres at least another year, fifth-graders on down. The really little kids — the kindergartners — had the most to gain from saving the tree. They'd attend Green Acres Elementary seven whole years. But they were too little to understand anything. They couldn't even read.

"You mean it, don't you?" Bruce said. "You really want to save that tree you're so crazy about." For once, he seemed — well, almost normal. He wasn't tripping her or calling her "Millie" or trying to catch cooties.

"That tree," Millicent replied, "happens to be my special place. But even if it wasn't, it shouldn't be cut down. My dad says that it's the biggest maple tree around here. The guy who built the houses in Maple Hills cut down all the old trees — " She stopped, suddenly remembering that Bruce lived in Maple Hills. "I mean, they're nice houses, but — "

"I know," he agreed. "The trees in our yard are all scrawny. My dad planted new trees, but it'll take years and years for them to grow. It takes a long time to grow a tree."

"Now you know why I have to save this tree," Millicent said earnestly. Just then the bell rang. The last stragglers hurried inside the building. Millicent tucked her sign under her arm and went in, too. Bruce actually opened the door for her. Or maybe he just got there first and decided not to slam it in her face.

In Mrs. Stann's room, Millicent and Bruce took their seats. They just made it before the tardy bell.

Roberta, who was hastily finishing her math homework, looked at the sign Millicent slid under her desk. "I saw you out there. How did it go?"

Millicent groaned. "Terrible. The big kids kept making fun of me. The others didn't pay any attention. It was worse than that time I set up a Kool-Aid stand."

"Poor location," Roberta said matter-of-factly. "When you start a business, location is everything."

"Well, it couldn't be location this time. I stood right in front of the school. Everybody could see me!"

"I didn't mean your protest," Roberta said. "I was thinking about your Kool-Aid stand. Nobody comes down our street, except the people who live there. You should have set your stand up in Maple Hills."

"My protest campaign is turning out a lot like my Kool-Aid stand," she said glumly. "And my miracles. Nothing I do ever turns out right. I wish I knew why."

Roberta summed it up for her. "You need help, Millicent. You can't run a protest all by yourself."

"I *have* to do this by myself. It wouldn't be one person making a difference if everybody got in the act. This is the only miracle I can give my father."

"It's not really a miracle," Roberta said. "You're just keeping a tree from being cut down. That's not a thing of wonder that can't be explained."

"It'll be a miracle if I *do* it," Millicent insisted. "And it's the only thing that will make my father feel better again."

"I think you just want all the credit," Roberta accused.

Millicent gazed out the window. It would be wonderful to go around and say, "See that tree? I saved it from the ax, all by myself. If it weren't for me, that tree would be somebody's firewood."

The maple tree stood grandly in the morning sunlight, lifting its branches toward the blue sky. The orange ribbon fluttered menacingly in the wind. Roberta was right. If she wanted to save the tree, really save it, she would have to accept help. But she'd be *chief* of the Save-the-Tree campaign.

"OK," she finally relented. "After school today I'm going to make more posters. You can help me. Be thinking of some good slogans."

Roberta looked happy. "I'll bring my art stuff over to your house this afternoon. I have lots of poster board."

"It's not going to work," Sheila said, watching Millicent write "Save Our Tree" in big letters with a Magic Marker.

"Who asked you?" Millicent didn't feel like putting up with Sheila's negative attitude.

Sheila had followed her brother to Millicent's house. Craig and Rudy were playing with their Matchbox cars while Millicent and Roberta lettered posters. Uninvited, Sheila slouched in a chair and made disparaging remarks.

"Nobody wants to save a tree," she said.

"You don't know that," Millicent said, about to lose her temper. "Why don't you quit whining and help us?"

Sheila slid off the chair. "Doing what?"

"Can you draw a tree? A nice tree?" Millicent gave her a poster to illustrate.

"Hey," Craig yelled, hating to be left out of anything. "I want to help."

"Me, too," Rudy piped.

"OK," Millicent told them. "Rudy, you and Craig color the letters."

Soon the five of them were making posters. Millicent silently congratulated herself on getting the two worst kids in the neighborhood to help with her campaign.

By suppertime they had completed twelve posters, brightly lettered and illustrated with Sheila's trees. Sheila came up with a good slogan, "Save a Tree and Save the Future." She really wasn't so bad, Millicent thought, when she wasn't whining.

She surveyed the array of posters leaning against the walls and furniture. "Everybody will join our cause now."

The next morning, Millicent met Roberta on the sidewalk in front of her house. She carried the posters, which were tied with twine so they'd stay in a neat bundle.

"We have to get to school extra early," she declared as they set off, "and hang these posters before the first bell."

"What does your mother think about your campaign?" Roberta asked. "I mean, being the head of the playground committee and all. She must be mad at you."

"No, she isn't. She believes in freedom of speech. She said something about freedom of speech and the right of aliens."

"Boy, if your mother believes in aliens having rights, she ought to realize the tree has rights, too."

"She really thinks we'd rather have this fancy

climber in our playground instead of a tree. She tries," Millicent added generously.

The school was open. Mr. Burke, the custodian, was sweeping the front hall. When he learned they intended to hang posters, he found them a roll of masking tape.

Millicent was taping the last poster on the wall by Mrs. Stann's room when Bruce and Lorenzo came up.

Bruce studied the sign critically.

"I suppose you're going to say it's crooked," Millicent said sarcastically.

"No, it's straight," Lorenzo said. "It's a nice poster."

Bruce still hadn't made any comment, which was unusual for him. Millicent couldn't stand the suspense. "Well," she demanded, "what's wrong with our posters?"

"Nothing's wrong with your posters. It's just that — a few posters aren't going to do much."

"We made twelve," Roberta said. "How many *should* we have made?"

Lorenzo said tactfully, "I think what Bruce means is that people will read your posters, but they won't think much about them. You know?"

"You have to make this a *real* campaign," Bruce said to Millicent. "Or else nobody'll pay attention. Watch when the buses start unloading. You'll see what I mean."

The first students trickled into the school. As Bruce predicted, they stopped to read Millicent's posters, but instead of reacting as Millicent hoped, they drifted into their classrooms, talking about the television shows they'd seen the night before. Nobody cared about Millicent's cause.

"What's the *matter* with them?" Millicent said in anguish. "All that work for nothing."

"See?" Bruce said, although without an I-told-you-so tone. "It's not enough. What are they supposed to do about your tree? How can they save it? You have to tell them."

"I don't know how to save the tree myself," Millicent admitted, discouraged. She was no good at this. She felt like giving up.

"You could have a petition for them to sign," Lorenzo suggested.

Roberta clutched Millicent's arm. "A petition! Didn't Geneva tell you a whole lot of signatures can sometimes change a law?"

"I forgot about petitions," Millicent said, brightening. "I'll make one right this minute." Digging her notebook out of her knapsack, she ripped out a sheet of looseleaf paper. "Does anybody have a pencil? I lost mine."

"You can't write a petition just like that," Bruce said.

"Why not?"

"Because. You have to plan things. That's the trouble with your campaign. You haven't planned anything." He glanced down the hall. "Here comes Mrs. Stann. We'll meet during recess and talk about this."

He went inside with Lorenzo.

Millicent glared after him. "The nerve of him! Who does he think he is? This is *my* campaign. *I* thought of saving the tree. And now Bruce wants to take over."

"Maybe he'll have some good ideas," Roberta said. "I think we need all the help we can get. But he is kind of pushy."

"Well, Bruce Johnston isn't going to push *me* around," Millicent said determinedly. "I didn't ask for his help." Secretly, though, she was glad Bruce and Lorenzo were on her side. The more kids who wanted to help, the better, so long as she remained chief.

At lunch, Bruce produced his campaign strategy. "Instead of one petition," he said, "we ought to have a bunch. And we should get other kids to take petitions around their neighborhoods."

Millicent liked his idea, but she wished she'd thought of it first. "Why would other people care about what happens to our tree? Grown-ups don't even go to school."

"Our parents care," Lorenzo said. "They're raising money for our new playground."

Then Roberta said, "How will we get kids interested enough to go around with petitions? They barely read our posters."

"We ought to have some kind of a meeting," Bruce said.

"A rally!" Millicent cried. "We'll hold a Save-the-Tree rally! Right under the tree! It'd be perfect."

Bruce shook his head doubtfully. "I don't know if the principal would let a mob of kids go outside."

He was probably right, but Millicent clung to the idea. "How about a rally *in*doors?" she said. "An assembly. We're always having assemblies about fire safety and stuff. Suppose we hold an assembly of our own?"

Bruce punched her on the arm. "Way to go, Millie. An assembly! That way we can tell the whole school!"

"What are we going to say?" Lorenzo asked. He was shy in front of an audience. He always mumbled his oral book reports. "We can't just stand up there on the stage and say 'Save our tree.' "

"I know! We'll put on a skit!" Now that she was inspired by other people's enthusiasm, Millicent's head teemed with ideas.

"A skit?" Roberta echoed.

"Yeah! We'll make it funny, because people like to laugh. But we'll make it sad, too, so they'll care about the tree."

They all agreed, although practical Roberta pointed out that they'd need permission from their teacher and the principal.

After lunch, the four of them clamored around Mrs. Stann's desk and told her their plan. She thought it was a wonderful cause, and even offered to clear it with the principal for them.

The principal gave them permission to hold the assembly on one condition, that he approve the script for their skit first. The date of the assembly was set for a week away.

Bruce said they should all work on the skit together, but Millicent stubbornly insisted on doing it alone.

"It's my idea," she said for the tenth time. "If you don't like it, Bruce, you can quit the campaign."

He stared at her. Millicent stared back. She didn't really want Bruce to quit. Much as she hated to admit it, she needed him.

"You aren't the only person with ideas," Bruce finally said. Millicent won that round.

At home, she went to her room. Taking a clean sheet of paper, she wrote at the top, "Archeologist from Outer Space Visits Our School." She copied the spelling of "archeologist" from a crumpled homework assignment in Abby's wastebasket. Bruce would probably want to be the archeologist from outer space, she thought, scribbling the cast list. He'd make a terrific alien.

# 11

"I made a copy for each of us." Millicent nervously passed handwritten copies of her skit to Lorenzo, Roberta, and Bruce.

The four of them were gathered around the kitchen table in Millicent's house. She had asked the others to come over to review her skit and make changes. Or rewrite it if nobody liked it. She crossed her fingers that that wouldn't happen.

"The idea came from my sister Abby," she confessed. "She has to do this report in her anthropology class. I thought it would make a neat skit. I hope you like it."

They began reading. Bruce snorted once, probably at the title of the skit. Millicent sat back in her chair, then sat forward again. She couldn't relax. This was worse than having the teacher read her book report out loud in class.

Bruce, who was a fast reader, finished first. He looked at Millicent. "You made me the guy from the future. The archeologist?"

"I thought you'd be a good archeologist," Millicent said sinkingly. Millicent was sure he didn't like it. None of them liked it. They were trying to figure out a way to tell her the skit was awful without hurting her feelings.

"You made me the tree," Lorenzo said. "Think I'd make a good tree?" He leaped up and struck a treelike pose.

"At least you're not the climber," Roberta said in a faintly complaining tone. "I don't do anything except hold my arms up. You get to die."

"But you're onstage more than Lorenzo," Millicent said. "I thought you'd like that. Lorenzo gets chopped down and dragged away and that's it for him. The climber is a very important part."

Bruce flipped through the pages. "I notice you gave yourself the most lines, Millie. You're the narrator."

"Somebody has to tell the audience what's going on," Millicent said defensively. "But I stand off to one side. Nobody will hardly even look at me." That wasn't true and Millicent knew it. The narrator's role was really the most important part. At the end of the skit, she'd recite the final plea to save the maple tree. She wanted people to leave the auditorium with her last words ringing in their ears.

"I like it," Bruce pronounced. "I think it's good."

"So do I," Lorenzo said. Millicent was afraid the only reason he agreed with Bruce was because he always went along with everything Bruce said. But he sounded sincere.

She looked at Roberta. Her best friend would be her harshest critic.

"I think," Roberta declared softly, "that we'd better have lots of petitions ready. After our skit, the whole school will want to save our tree."

Millicent grinned. It was a go! Tomorrow they would show the skit to the principal for approval. And in four days, they would perform the skit before the entire student body of Green Acres Elementary.

Not only did the principal approve Millicent's skit, but he also allowed the members of the Save-the-Tree campaign to use the mimeograph machine in the office to run off petitions to pass out at the end of the assembly.

Signatures from everyone in the school would be great, but Millicent wanted a *mountain* of names to present to the playground committee. The maple tree didn't just belong to the students of Green Acres Elementary — the tree belonged to the whole community.

At home, Mrs. Adams was aware of every detail of Millicent's campaign. Millicent felt a little funny talking about her plans at the supper table, since her mother was the enemy, sort of. But both her parents supported her one hundred percent.

"Always do what you feel is right," Mrs. Adams told Millicent one night at dinner. "Even if it's not the popular thing to do."

"These kids are really going to show your committee," Mr. Adams remarked, buttering a roll. "You better be prepared to move that climber thing somewhere else."

"We'll wait for the results of Millicent's assembly," Mrs. Adams said. "I can't make changes on the strength of promises. Millicent and her friends will have to deliver enough signatures to convince my committee and the PTA that it will be worth the expense to have the architect's plans redesigned. And maybe delay the opening of the new playground. The students will have to know this, too. Many of them are eager for a new playground."

Milllcent's stomach fluttered. She never realized the entire impact of her campaign. Suppose the students decided not to sign because they'd rather have the new playground open on time?

After supper Abby went to the movies with a friend, Rudy settled down in front of the TV, and Millicent and her mother busied themselves with their committee work. Left alone, Mr. Adams retreated to his study. Millicent was suddenly reminded of the real reason she was working so hard to save the maple tree. If her campaign worked, her father would see that one person — the chief of the Save-the-Tree campaign — could still make a difference. He would realize the world could be changed, a tree at a time. They just *had* to win.

From the side of the stage, partially hidden by the velvet curtain, Millicent watched the sixth-graders file into the auditorium and fill the back rows. She wiped her damp palms on her skirt. They were almost ready to begin. The students were seated according to grade, the front rows occupied by giggling, piping-voiced kindergartners. Now that the sixth-graders were there, it would only be a matter of seconds before Mr. Dwight, the principal, announced the program.

Millicent glanced at Roberta and Lorenzo behind her. Lorenzo acted even more nervous than she felt. He looked like he wanted to walk off the stage and never come back. Roberta shook her black bangs, a signal she was a little anxious, too.

Only Bruce appeared calm. Paying no attention to the crowd just beyond the curtain, he adjusted the shoulder straps of the cardboard spaceship he'd made to "crash-land" in. It was a neat spaceship, a carton spray-painted silver with a foil bubble on top. The carton slipped over Bruce's head, resting on the shoulder straps so he could ditch it quickly to look like a crash landing.

Millicent knew he made the spaceship so his entrance would be dramatic and memorable. She didn't really like it, since none of the rest of them had props. It was hard to be the chief over somebody like Bruce, who clearly *did* have ideas of his own.

"There's your mother," Roberta said, leaning forward. "And mine. They must have come together."

Millicent watched Mrs. Stann guide her mother

and Mrs. Holloway to seats that had been saved for them. Bruce's and Lorenzo's mothers both worked and weren't able to take off to see the skit. More than anything, Millicent wished her father could be there. The whole assembly was really for him.

"Here comes Mr. Dwight," Lorenzo croaked, his face pale.

Millicent's knees weakened, but she felt it was her duty as chief to give the others a pep talk.

"Don't worry," she reassured him. "You'll be fine. Just remember not to fall over too soon. Don't die before I tell you to."

"I'm going to die right now," Lorenzo moaned as Mr. Dwight took the podium.

"Line up," Millicent commanded. She squared her shoulders, ready to go onstage first. Lorenzo got behind her, then Roberta, and last, Bruce, lugging his silver carton.

Mr. Dwight welcomed the students, then introduced the program.

"Four students from Mrs. Stann's fourth-grade class have worked very hard on the presentation you are about to enjoy," he said. "Please show them your best Green Acres manners." The principal stepped back from the lectern to polite clapping.

Now that her moment of going onstage had actually arrived, Millicent was petrified. It was one thing to talk about being brave — it was another thing to *be* brave.

On trembling legs, she forced herself to walk across the stage to the podium. Placing her script on the tilted surface of the lectern, she faced the audience, a sea of swimming faces. Everyone in the packed auditorium was staring at her, waiting for her to say something. The little kids in the front rows squirmed in their seats, already restless. Some kids snickered and someone bellowed, "Speech! Speech!"

A strange feeling swept over Millicent, a thick-tongued wooden sensation. She was afraid she'd never move again, much less be able to narrate her skit. The microphone terrified her. She'd never used one before. When they had rehearsed the skit, the microphone had been turned off.

She probably would have stood there forever if Roberta hadn't darted out and jostled Millicent's elbow.

"*Say* something," Roberta hissed. "The paper is right in front of you." She ran back to her place behind the curtain, amid more laughter.

Millicent dragged her eyes from the packed auditorium to the neatly copied narrative on the lectern.

"This is the story of a tree," she began, her mouth too close to the microphone. The *s*'s and *t*'s exploded in electronic buzzes. More laughter. From her delivery or the actual words, Millicent didn't know. A couple of teachers rose to direct a few warning looks. The laughter subsided.

She started over, this time not so close to the microphone. "This is the story of a tree. Long, long ago, a bird flying over dropped a seed on the ground. The seed became a tiny plant. Lots of sun and rain made the plant grow into a sturdy tree. The tree loved being a tree. Birds built nests in its branches. People sat in its shade when they were hot. Sometimes the tree was lonely, like in the winter, but it knew it was important, and that made it happy again."

It was time for Lorenzo to make his appearance.

She braved a quick glance at the audience. The little kids wriggled, probably bored. Too much talking, she figured, and not enough action. She wished she'd thought of that when she wrote the skit.

Lorenzo had missed his cue.

Millicent said again, "Sometimes the tree was lonely, but it knew it was important and THAT MADE IT HAPPY."

Two hands pushed a reluctant Lorenzo from the wing. He stumbled across the stage, bringing more giggles, and took his place to the right of Millicent. He raised his arms and tried to look like a happy tree. Millicent thought he looked more like a nervous boy with his arms stuck up in the air.

She continued. "Some people came and built a school right next to the tree. Little children played around the tree during recess. The tree was very happy. The tree believed everyone loved it. But it was wrong. One day a man came and chopped it down."

Lorenzo's legs buckled and he hit the stage like a toppled skyscraper.

"They took the tree away," Millicent said, remembering too late they had changed the script and left that line out. Millicent decided a dead tree lying on the stage would be a more powerful symbol than to have the tree hauled away. Besides, they were short an actor to drag Lorenzo away.

"Uh — " she stammered. Lorenzo was crawling uncertainly offstage. Millicent was mortified. Dead trees did not crawl offstage by themselves.

"They left the tree to rot!" she screeched. In an undertone she said to Lorenzo, "Lie back down!" He halted in mid-crawl and fell again, a dead tree once more.

Kids were laughing openly now. So were some teachers, Millicent noted miserably. Her play was going all wrong!

Valiantly, she read on. "The people built a climber in place of the tree."

Roberta marched onstage and held her arms straight out, pretending to be a climber. Millicent thought she smiled too much for a piece of playground equipment.

"Children climbed on the climber. But the birds couldn't nest there. And people couldn't sit under it for shade. Years and years and years go by.

The school is empty. The playground is very quiet."

The audience was also quiet, listening attentively.

"One day a stranger arrived from outer space," she said, her voice strong.

Bruce hurled himself onstage, collapsing in a heap near the climber. He struggled out of his cardboard spaceship, looking dazed. Roberta kicked the silver carton with her foot. She didn't want any prop keeping the audience from seeing her.

"The stranger was from another planet. He was a scientist and he'd been sent to Earth to study the old civilization." Abby helped her with that part. It sounded good.

"The buildings were empty, so the scientist had to figure out what they had been used for."

Bruce, who had been examining the walls of the stage, turned to scrutinize Roberta. Roberta began giggling.

"He figured out this building was once a school, and a playground, but he didn't know what the climber was." Bruce shrugged with exaggerated puzzlement. "Finally he decided it was an *artificial* tree for children to climb on. He wondered where the real trees were. Why did the Earth children have to play on artificial trees? On his planet there were nice, natural trees that everybody loved. The stranger was sad for the Earth children."

Bruce looked like he'd lost his best friend. Roberta couldn't stop giggling. Millicent wanted to choke them both. Why did everybody have to ham it up? This was *important* — a tree's life was at stake.

It was time for her final speech. She waited a moment, making sure everyone was looking at her.

"The tree is the big maple tree right outside the fourth-grade classrooms," she said. "You all know it. It's been here for fifty years, way before our school. But it's going to be cut down for the new playground. A climber will be put in its place." She paused, letting her statement sink in.

"Some of us want to save the maple tree. It gives us shade in the summer, and pretty colored leaves in the fall. It gives birds perches in the winter, and it gives all of us hope in the spring when the buds come out. We could adopt the tree as our school mascot. We could take care of it and study it for science. The maple tree deserves to live. Won't you help save it?"

Her final words rang out, just as she imagined they would. The auditorium was completely silent. Millicent's heart plummeted. Her skit hadn't worked! They hated it, they were all bored, asleep probably. She wanted to cry.

A few hesitant claps sounded here and there. Then the clapping branched out, like the maple tree, until the auditorium thundered with applause.

Mr. Dwight stepped forward and took the microphone again. "Let's thank Millicent Adams, Roberta Holloway, Lorenzo Scrementi, and Bruce Johnston for their wonderful presentation. You were terrific, all of you." The applause swelled appreciably. Millicent grinned at Roberta.

"There are copies of petitions at the doors," Mr. Dwight said. "Please pick up one on your way out if you want to join Millicent and her friends' campaign. I know I'm going to be the first to sign a petition."

As the classes were dismissed, Millicent was amazed to see kids literally fighting for copies of the petition. Tears stung her eyes. She had done it. No, *they* had done it.

She couldn't have put on the assembly without the help of Bruce, Lorenzo, and Roberta. Being the chief wasn't such a great position. Without other people, a chief is just a person.

Maybe, Millicent thought, it took teamwork to change the world. Maybe one person couldn't make a difference. But a lot of people could.

# 12

With a gold fountain pen, Mrs. Taylor signed her full name — Alma Norton Duffill Taylor — on the first line of Millicent's petition. Millicent watched admiringly. She never knew Mrs. Taylor had so many names.

"There." Mrs. Taylor added a fancy flourish under her signature. "I seldom sign petitions, but this one is for an excellent cause."

"Thanks." Millicent folded her petition and put it in her coat pocket. "Nobody'll sign my petition as good as you have." One of Mrs. Taylor's Persian cats came to rub around Millicent's ankles. She bent to pet it. The cat lifted a paw and daintily washed one ear, turning it inside out into a pink triangle. Millicent laughed. "He acts like I got him dirty!"

Mrs. Taylor gave her cat a fond glance. "He thinks you did. Mike is fussy, but very sweet."

"Too bad I can't sign your cats' names on my petition," Millicent said. "Mike Taylor, Allison Taylor, Greta Taylor — I'd fill the whole page. But that wouldn't be honest."

"You won't have any trouble getting signatures," Mrs. Taylor maintained. "Your cause is a worthy one. And such an original approach. Adopting a tree for the community. Everyone will love the idea."

"If we make the tree our school mascot," Millicent said, never tiring of explaining her plan, "the students of Green Acres will look out for the tree, take care of it. And we can use it for science. You know, study leaves and birds and bugs. Dad said we could study history with it, too, all the things the tree has lived through, like the Depression and World War Two. But mostly, the tree will be there for everyone to enjoy." She liked that part the best, knowing the tree would bring pleasure to the next student who sat at her desk in Mrs. Stann's class.

"You've worked very hard," Mrs. Taylor acknowledged. "It will pay off, you'll see."

"Keep your fingers crossed. Well, I'd better go now. Dad promised he'd take me and Rudy to the supermarket this afternoon, so we can stand outside and get people to sign our petitions."

Mrs. Taylor walked her to the door. "Your sister's baby should be here soon, shouldn't it?"

In the excitement of the Save-the-Tree campaign, Millicent had temporarily forgotten about Geneva's baby. "Oh, yeah, I guess. The nursery is all ready, for whenever the baby gets here."

With the Saturday afternoon crowds at the grocery store, it didn't take Millicent thirty minutes to fill her petitions with signatures. Rudy was finished even sooner. He was too shy to explain what the petition was for — he merely held out the pen and looked up at the person with big winsome eyes.

The deadline for the petitions was six o'clock that evening. Mrs. Adams had called a special meeting of the playground committee. Millicent, Roberta, Bruce, and Lorenzo would turn in the petitions. Then the committee would discuss the fate of the maple tree.

The day before, on Friday, Mrs. Stann presented Millicent with a sheaf of petitions that had circulated through the classes. Everybody in the entire school, including the secretaries in the main office, the custodians, and the cafeteria ladies, signed Millicent's petition. They all wanted to save the tree.

"How many signatures do you think we'll need?" Millicent asked her father on the way home from the store. "A hundred? A thousand? A million? Geneva said you needed a lot of names to change a law."

"I don't believe any certain number is required to get the playground committee to change their minds," Mr. Adams allowed. "The idea is to have a lot of signatures. Enough to convince the committee that people want the tree."

Her father had been a big help with the petitions. When Sheila and Craig and Rudy tried to obtain signatures from the same houses on Wagner Avenue, Mr. Adams settled the dispute by suggesting that Sheila take her petition to her Girl Scout troop, Craig take his to his Cub Scout troop, and Rudy, who was in the same Cub Scout troop, could have the neighborhood. Mr. Adams even took a petition to work and got signatures. "People like to save things like trees," he commented. "It makes them feel good."

Millicent hoped that saving the maple tree would make her father feel good. It was the only miracle she had left.

At home, Abby handed Millicent five more petitions, dropped off by Green Acres students. Two of the sheets were filled with signatures, the other three only partially filled.

It was two-thirty. Three and half more hours till the meeting at the school. Roberta, Bruce, and Lorenzo were bringing their petitions to Millicent's house. From there they would all go to Green Acres for the meeting. Millicent was starting to feel nervous.

Mrs. Adams came out of her room at a quarter to six, wearing her purple PTA suit. Millicent gulped — her mother meant business when she wore that suit.

"I'll see you and your friends in a few minutes," she told Millicent, getting into her coat. She smiled and brushed Millicent's cheek with a kiss. "Don't look so scared, honey. There's nothing to be afraid of. It'll be fine, however it turns out. I'll still be your mother, and you'll still be my little girl. By the way, I'm very proud of you."

Millicent hugged her mother. "Thanks, Mom."

Her mother hugged her back, then clasped her hand. "Good luck, Millicent."

"Good luck, Mom." She shook her mother's hand solemnly. Her mother was right. However the project turned out, they were still family.

Mrs. Adams left, driving Mr. Adams' car to the meeting. The station wagon was reserved for the Save-the-Tree campaign members.

Bruce and Lorenzo arrived first. Bruce's hair had been slicked down for the occasion, and he had on regular pants instead of jeans. Lorenzo looked neat as always.

"I got both my petitions filled," Bruce said, handing Millicent the dog-eared pages.

"So did I." Lorenzo gave her his petitions. "We went over to my grandmother's and I got people in her apartment building to sign it."

Millicent put the petitions in a special folder her father had given her. "Where's Roberta? How can she be late — she lives right across the street."

At that moment, the doorbell rang twice, sharply. Roberta stood on the porch, breathless with excitement. "We went to the mall. I got fifty-two signatures!"

The folder was impressively thick. They exclaimed over the number of names — so many people they didn't even know who wanted to help save their maple tree.

"OK, let's go." Mr. Adams jingled the car keys.

"I'm sitting up front!" Bruce yelled. "Me, too!" Lorenzo seconded.

Millicent poked Roberta, stifling a giggle. The four of them had worked together on the campaign, performed in a skit and everything, but the boys still didn't want to sit next to the girls.

At Green Acres Elementary, Millicent was surprised to see most of the parking spots in the visitors' lot occupied by cars. All these people just to talk about a tree? Then she remembered her mother saying the committee had other things to discuss, besides the tree. The bulldozers were coming next week to begin clearing the new playground and the committee had several loose ends to tie up.

They milled around the chilly parking lot, stamping their feet to keep warm. Bruce opened his mouth wide, his breath making frosty puffs in the air.

Mr. Adams checked his watch. "They ought to be through the preliminary stuff by now. We can go in. Millicent, do you have the folder?"

Millicent felt a stab of panic. "The folder! I don't have it! I left it at home!"

"It's right under your arm!" Roberta said, giggling. Bruce and Lorenzo laughed.

They went inside the school. The hallway

seemed eerie and quiet. Millicent realized with a start that the building was always like that when school wasn't in session. It occurred to her that school wasn't a building or even a place — it was teachers and students. They could have school anywhere, even under the maple tree outside, and it would still be school, although the building made it much nicer.

The playground committee was meeting in one of the sixth-grade classrooms at the end of the hall. "We'd meet in the first-grade rooms because they are closest to the door, but the seats are too little!" Mrs. Adams remarked with a laugh.

The door was open. Murmuring voices rose and fell. Millicent, who had been leading the way, suddenly stopped. Her father gently took her elbow.

"It's all right," he urged. "Go on in. They're expecting you."

Hesitantly, Millicent walked into the classroom. The others followed. The committee had arranged chairs in a circle near the blackboard. Mrs. Adams was at the board, writing some figures. When she saw Millicent, she smiled.

"Come in, please," she told them. "Everyone, these are the members of the Save-the-Tree campaign." She introduced them by name. "They've worked very hard and now they have something for us."

Millicent stood first on one foot, then the other. As the group's spokesperson, she was supposed to give a little speech. She was just as nervous as she'd been during the assembly. Bruce muttered, "*Say* something."

She held out the folder to her mother. "Here are the petitions we had people sign. There are a lot of names. Everybody wants to leave the tree in our playground."

Mrs. Adams took the folder. "Millicent, tell us what you plan to do with the tree, if it's saved."

Millicent gave her mother a grateful glance. Her mother was making it easy for her. "Our school will adopt the tree, you know, like a mascot. We'll study it and take care of it. But everybody can enjoy it, even if you don't go to school. It'll belong to the community."

The committee members were smiling and nodding. Millicent hoped they weren't just being polite to a bunch of kids.

"Thank you, all," Mrs. Adams said, dismissing the Save-the-Tree campaigners. "We'll take up this matter right now. When we have a vote, we'll let you know."

Millicent filed out with Bruce, Lorenzo, and Roberta. They walked down to the library to wait for the committee's decision. Roberta took a book off the shelf, but Millicent was too keyed up to read.

"After all our work, suppose they decide to chop the tree down anyway?" she said.

Her father patted her hand. "You will have tried your best. That's what you have to remember. You didn't quit."

Millicent tried to find some consolation in his words. She wanted to tell him she did it all for him, to make him see that one person — well, one person and some of her friends — could make a difference in the world. If they lost, she was afraid her father would stay down in the dumps forever.

Fifteen minutes later, a woman on Mrs. Adams' committee appeared at the library door. "We've reached a verdict," she said cheerfully.

Bruce bolted from his chair. He and Lorenzo ran to the sixth-grade room, but Millicent was too anxious to run. When she walked into the room, her mother was grinning.

"The tree stays," she said simply. "We have decided that your enthusiasm and the weight of these signatures were just too overwhelming."

The Save-the-Tree campaign members cheered. Bruce whistled shrilly.

Mrs. Adams held up her hand. "Since the maple tree will remain on the playground, we have decided to cancel the climber. It was too big to put anywhere else. Instead, we're going to build a merry-go-round for the younger children. Congratulations. You all did a marvelous job."

The committee still had other business to discuss, so Millicent and the others left. Outside, Millicent cried, "We won! We won!" Her voice rang out over the frosty parking lot.

"Yes," her father said. "You won. How about hamburgers at McDonald's to celebrate?"

McDonald's was crowded and noisy but Millicent didn't care. She felt like sharing her news with the whole world. Her father bought them all hamburgers, french fries, and Cokes. Millicent bit happily into her juicy sandwich. Nothing had ever tasted so delicious in her entire life.

"Thanks, Mr. Adams," Lorenzo said. "This is really nice of you."

"Victories come along rarely — they deserve to be celebrated," Mr. Adams said. He hadn't ordered any food, only a cup of coffee which he sipped thoughtfully.

"I can't wait to go back to school Monday," Bruce declared. "Can you imagine how great it'll be when everybody hears we saved the tree? We'll be heroes!" Bruce took out a stub of pencil and doodled a star on a stack of napkins. He scribbled the word "Hero" in the center of each star and passed one to each of them.

Millicent tucked her napkin in her pocket. She wasn't sure why, but she wanted to keep Bruce's napkin.

He still called her Millie now and then, but he hadn't tripped her or knocked her down in quite a while. Maybe Bruce was becoming a friend. He was like Roberta — he didn't do everything Millicent told him to, or agree with everything she said. Millicent liked friends who kept her on her toes. It made life interesting.

"I just remembered," Bruce said, sputtering

Coke. "We don't go to school Wednesday! It's a teachers' work day. How do you like that? I've been so busy with this tree stuff, I forgot about the teachers' work day."

"We have a Valentine's party on Thursday," Roberta said.

The boys made faces. "Valentines," Bruce said. "Yuck."

"I think we ought to make a sign for our tree," Millicent suggested. "So everybody'll know it's ours."

Roberta nodded. "Good idea. But what will it say?"

Millicent nudged her father's arm. "What do you think, Daddy? What should the sign say?"

"I don't know, pumpkin. You four have been pretty involved with this project — you'll come up with something, I'm sure."

He spoke lightly, but his eyes had a faraway look, as if he wished he were somewhere else.

"Daddy," Millicent said. "Aren't you glad we saved the tree? Aren't you glad it isn't going to be cut down?"

"Of course, I'm glad. The tree ought to be thrilled, too."

The others laughed at his remark, but Millicent felt her own happiness dampen. He was still down in the dumps.

It wasn't enough, she realized sadly. They had worked so hard to save the tree and had *won*, but their victory still wasn't enough to cheer up her father.

Maybe he was right, she thought. Maybe one person — or even a bunch of people working together — didn't really matter. They had saved the maple tree, that was true, but the world was still the same place. Nothing had changed.

# 13

Millicent wasn't sure what woke her. It wasn't her alarm. She hadn't even set it the night before because the next day was a teachers' work day, a no-school day. And Abby didn't make a lot of noise starting her little yellow car to leave for George Mason University. In fact, it was very quiet, both inside and outside, but mostly outside.

She sat up and pulled up her shade. Fine white crystals brushed gently against the windowpane. It was snowing.

Snow! At long last!

The snow must have just started because the ground was barely white in patches, but the sky was gray and flat. It was going to snow more than those tiny white flakes whispering against her window.

Millicent leaped out of bed and ran to Rudy's room. "Snow!" she shrieked, flinging open his door. "Get up! It's snowing!"

"Snow?" Rudy replied from the depths of his pillow. "Real live snow?"

"Real live snow. Better get up before it's all

gone." Laughing, Millicent skipped out to the kitchen. Her father and Abby had already left for work and college. Mrs. Adams was writing a list.

"Mom, it's snowing! Our first snow! Isn't it exciting?"

"Well, it's pretty," Mrs. Adams said reluctantly. Like most grown-ups, she considered snow a problem, especially to drive in. "But the weatherman promised it will clear up by ten or so. Maybe just an inch or two. I have too much to do today to fight bad weather." She got up to make Millicent's breakfast.

Millicent gazed dreamily out the window. She couldn't wait to go outside. "I wish we didn't have a teachers' work day today. I wish it was a snow day."

"You have off anyway. I don't know why you children always love snow days. You forget you have to make them up at the end of the year, in the summer, when the weather is nice."

Summer was too far off to worry about, as far as Millicent was concerned. The snow was falling today, right now, and she wanted to take full advantage of it and that included getting off from school because of the weather, not because the teachers had to write out report cards.

"I'm going outside, Mom," a voice called from the hall. "I'll eat breakfast when I get back."

"Rudy Adams, come back here!" Mrs. Adams ordered. Rudy walked into the kitchen. He wore his jacket over his pajamas and had crammed his slippered feet into rubber boots. He carried his new snow saucer like a shield. "I thought so," Mrs. Adams said, smiling. "Rudy, it's too early to go out. And you're not dressed properly."

"Yeah," Millicent put in. "You haven't got a hat on."

"But, Mom, it's *snowing*!" he wailed. "I have to hurry before it melts. First, I have to slide down Mrs. Taylor's hill, then I have to make a snowman, and then — "

"First, you're going to eat breakfast." Mrs. Adams set a bowl of oatmeal at his place. "Eat your cereal and I'll make cinnamon toast for both of you."

As they munched crispy toast triangles, Mrs. Adams outlined their day. She had to go downtown to buy fresh fish for the neighborhood food co-op. And she wanted to stop and see Geneva in Maryland. Millicent was torn. She'd love to see her sister, but she'd rather stay home and play in the snow.

Rudy felt the same way. "Can't we stay here?" he asked plaintively. "Me and Millicent will be OK."

"I'll be gone all morning. The highways are going to be slow and busy with this snow," Mrs. Adams said. "We need to get moving. You and Millicent can play in the snow this afternoon, when we come back."

Rudy looked dismayed. "It might be all gone."

"It won't be gone," Mrs. Adams promised. "The

temperature is just above freezing. The snow will stick around, I'm sure. Come on, kids, get dressed. Let's go see Geneva."

As Mrs. Adams predicted, traffic was heavy and slow on the Beltway to Maryland. It took them over an hour to drive thirty miles. "People around here go crazy whenever a flake of snow falls from the sky," Mrs. Adams complained. "I bet the stores are mobbed with people buying bread and milk. By tonight, there won't be a drop of milk or a crumb of bread left in the entire Washington area."

Millicent pictured empty shelves in the grocery stores and people's carts piled high with nothing but loaves of bread and cartons of milk. Why did they buy bread and milk when it snowed? she wondered. Why not candy bars or potato chips? If she were going to be snowed in for any length of time, those were the things she wouldn't want to run out of, not bread and milk.

By the time they reached Geneva's apartment, the snow had tapered off a bit. Geneva's red Volkswagen Beetle, parked in front of her building, was covered with only a light powdery dusting. Maybe the snow wasn't going to amount to much after all.

Geneva met them at the door, her blue eyes wide with worry. "I knew this was going to happen!" she said to Mrs. Adams. "Why does it have to snow this week of all weeks!"

"Now, now," Mrs. Adams said soothingly. "The

forecasters say this snow may not be more than an inch or two. Most of the time, the big storms miss us."

"I hope not," said Rudy. "I want to use my snow saucer."

Geneva patted his head. "Hi, kids. I didn't mean to ignore you. I'm just a little frantic today."

"Is this the week you're going to the hospital?" Millicent asked, noting the suitcase by the door.

"I'm supposed to," Geneva replied. "But I don't know when exactly."

They took off their coats and Mrs. Adams made hot chocolate for everyone, with extra marshmallows. "The roads will be fine when you need to go to the hospital," she reassured Geneva. "You look tired. How are you feeling?"

"Edgy," Geneva said, listlessly dunking her marshmallows with the back of her spoon. "I woke up this morning feeling — I don't know. I can't describe it."

Her sister looked so pale and worried, Millicent felt sorry for her. She didn't really want to hog the favorite child position, not over Geneva. If Geneva wanted to be the favorite child, then it was OK with her.

"I had the same feeling," Millicent said, trying to make her feel better. "It was quiet, that's what I figured it was. And then I saw the snow."

Geneva smiled at her. Millicent noticed that there were blue shadows underneath her sister's eyes. "Maybe that's what it was. The snow. And the quiet."

Mrs. Adams glanced around the apartment. There were dishes from Lyman's breakfast piled in the sink and a basket of unfolded laundry on the floor. Dirty clothes were heaped by the washer.

"How would you like a helper for the day?" she offered Geneva. "I have to go downtown to buy fish for the co-op, but I could let Millicent stay here with you. I don't like leaving you alone when you're feeling tired. Millicent can do the dishes and fold laundry until I come back. You just take it easy."

"Hey, yeah!" Millicent loved the idea of helping her big sister for the day. "I'll fix you lunch on a tray and everything."

"Me, too," Rudy piped. "I want to help Geneva, too."

Mrs. Adams tactfully headed him off. "I need you to help me pick out fish. And don't you want to see the boats?"

Rudy looked torn, but the fishing boats won. "Mom needs me," he told Geneva regretfully. "I should go with her."

"Keep her out of trouble," Geneva laughed. "It looks like the snow is letting up a bit. You ought to go now, Mom, while you can. I think I want to lie down." She went into the bedroom next to the nursery to lie across the bed.

Mrs. Adams put a load of laundry in the washer and filled the sink with hot soapy water. As she eased the dishes into the sink, she gave Millicent instructions.

"I'm leaving you in charge, Millicent. Geneva is tired and worried, so don't chatter or bother her. Let her rest, OK? I'll be back as soon as I can."

"I'll be as quiet as a mouse," Millicent promised. "I'll tiptoe around the apartment. I won't even turn on the television."

Mrs. Adams handed Rudy his jacket and put her coat on again. She kissed Millicent on the cheek. "I'm counting on you, Millicent."

Millicent waved them out the door, then set to work. First she washed and dried the dishes. She didn't know which cupboards the dishes went in, but she didn't bother her sister. It took quite a while to put everything away and by then the laundry was done. Millicent efficiently loaded the laundry into the dryer and set the timer as she often did at home. Then she folded the clean laundry.

As she swept the kitchen floor, she congratulated herself. Here she was, a nine-year-old girl, taking care of an apartment and her twenty-two-year-old sister. She enjoyed her role so much, she dug out a cookbook from the rack next to the table and pored over the pages, looking for a tempting lunch treat to perk up her sister's appetite. The recipes were awfully hard, and Geneva probably didn't have most of the ingredients.

Millicent glanced at the clock. It was lunch time. Geneva had been sleeping for over an hour. She was probably hungry by now.

She tiptoed into the bedroom. The blinds were drawn; the room was gloomy and dark. Geneva was lying on top of the covers. Her eyes opened when she heard Millicent slip through the door.

"What time is it?" she said groggily, struggling to sit up.

"Almost one o'clock. Are you hungry? I'll fix you something to eat. What would you like?"

Geneva fell back against the pillows. "I don't know. I'm not really hungry. Fix yourself a sandwich. There's all kinds of stuff in the refrigerator."

Millicent was concerned about her sister. "You didn't eat any breakfast. I'll make you something really special, OK?"

"OK." Geneva's response was feeble, though she tried to smile.

Back in the kitchen, Millicent bustled around getting their lunch. She had been thinking of a new way of making peanut butter-and-jelly sandwiches. Last night, before she went to sleep, she worked this out in her mind. It ought to be yummy.

She made two peanut butter-and-jelly sandwiches the regular way, then spread butter on the outer pieces of bread and slid both sandwiches into the toaster oven. She adjusted the setting to "Broil." Digging a tray from beneath the counter, Millicent set the tray with napkins, half a bag of corn chips, a saucer with four Oreos, and two glasses of milk. The toaster oven gave a little "ding," to indicate the sandwiches were ready.

The whole kitchen smelled like cooked peanut butter, a very pleasant peanutty smell. The sandwiches were nice and brown, but slippery, Millicent discovered. Hot peanut butter squirted out around the edges.

She took the tray into the bedroom, sloshing the milk only a little. "Lunchtime!" she sang out, setting the tray on the end of the bed.

Geneva propped herself up against the pillows. "I really feel — oh, Millicent, what is that smell?"

"It's our lunch. I made grilled peanut butter-and-jelly sandwiches. Don't they look yummy?" She took her plate off the tray and balanced it across her knees, pushing the tray toward Geneva. "I would have put marshmallows on them, but Mom used them all in our hot chocolate. Too bad because they would have melted all gooey — "

Geneva moaned. "Millicent, I feel just awful. I don't think I can eat anything. Thanks, anyway, honey."

"Are you sick? I can't see in here — it's so dark." Millicent put her plate back on the tray and went over to the window. When she pulled up the venetian blinds, she gasped.

The cars in the parking lot below were buried

under mounds of snow. The sky was white with thickly falling flakes.

Her sister rolled over on her side, away from the light. "Oh, Millicent, I think I need to go to the hospital."

"Right now?" Millicent cried. "Right this minute?"

"It's OK," her sister said, laughing weakly. "Call Lyman at work. The number is on the pad by the phone in the kitchen. Just tell him I think it's time. He'll know what to do."

Millicent ran into the kitchen. On a notepad she saw "Flint Hill Prep School" and a long-distance phone number. Her brother-in-law taught English at the private school in Virginia.

With shaking fingers she dialed the number and asked for Lyman Renquist. After what seemed like an hour, Lyman came on the line.

"It's time!" Millicent squawked into the receiver. "Geneva says it's time! You have to take her to the hospital."

"Millicent?" Lyman said. "Is that you? Are you at our apartment?"

"It's a no-school day," she explained. "Mom wanted to see Geneva, but she had to go downtown to the fish market so she left me here to help Geneva take it easy and after I made grilled peanut butter-and-jelly sandwiches, Geneva said to tell you it's time. I did the dishes and a load of clothes all by myself," she added. Then, frantic again, "You have to hurry!"

"I'm on my way," Lyman said and hung up.

Millicent went back to the bedroom. "I called Lyman. He's on his way."

"Good." Geneva rolled over on her other side. "How's the weather? Is it still snowing? I hope he doesn't have any trouble."

It was snowing like crazy, but Millicent didn't tell Geneva. Instead she said, "Is there anything I can get you? Want me to make sure your suitcase is OK?"

"If you want. Get out my heavy winter coat, will you?"

Glad to be able to do something, Millicent galloped into the living room. She couldn't stop running. The very idea that her sister needed to get to the hospital filled Millicent with an urgency she'd never felt before. She took Geneva's coat out of the closet and laid it beside the suitcase. Then she went to the window to see if she could spot Lyman's car. She couldn't see anything but white — white parking lot, white humps with cars underneath, a white world.

The phone rang. Millicent snatched it like a life preserver. It was her brother-in-law.

"Millicent?" Lyman's voice was high and shrill. "How's Geneva?"

"She's OK, I guess. But I thought you'd be here! Where are you?"

"At work, still. My car won't start! A friend is lending me his, but that's not the half of it. I just heard there is an accident on the bridge and the

Beltway is blocked in both directions. Listen, Millicent. Call your mother and tell her to take Geneva to the hospital. I'll meet you there, okay?"

"Wait, Lyman — " He obviously forgot she had told him her mother and Rudy were at the fish market on Maine Avenue, in downtown D.C., miles and miles from there! Then Millicent remembered her mother's last words: "I'm counting on you, Millicent."

Her mother was counting on her. Geneva was counting on her. And now Lyman was counting on her. She couldn't let all those people down.

"Millicent? What is it?" Lyman was saying. "Is something wrong?"

"No," she fibbed. "Everything is fine. We'll see you at the hospital." She hung up, chewing her bottom lip.

She was scared.

Geneva needed to go to the hospital. Her mother was at a fish market on Maine Avenue, downtown, and the bridge was blocked, which meant that people trying to cross the Potomac River to go from Virginia to Maryland, or vice versa, were stuck. And it was snowing wildly. The big snow she'd been waiting for all winter was happening now. And her sister needed to get to the hospital.

It was too much responsibility for a nine-year-old girl. Too much for a newspaper mogul, even. She needed help.

There was only one person who could help them.

Millicent picked up the phone and dialed her father's number at the Labor Department where he worked. His secretary put him on the line immediately at the sound of her voice.

"Daddy!" Millicent screamed. "Geneva has to go to the hospital and Lyman can't get over the bridge and Mom is at the fish market. Will you come?" She began to cry.

"Hold on, pumpkin," her father said calmly. "You're at Geneva's apartment, right?"

"Yes," she sobbed.

"And Geneva needs to go to the hospital?"

"Yes!"

"Tell Geneva I'm on my way."

"But, Daddy — what about the snow?" The snow was ruining everything. Millicent hated herself for hoping for snow every day.

"I'll be there," he vowed.

Wiping her tears on her sleeve, Millicent went back into Geneva's bedroom. "Daddy's on his way," she reported.

"Daddy? What happened to Lyman?" Geneva asked.

Millicent related the chain of events to her sister, the snow, the blocked bridge, the car that wouldn't start.

To her surprise, Geneva started laughing. "I knew this would happen! Didn't I tell you? I just knew it would snow the day I had to go to the hospital!"

Millicent laughed, too. But then they both stopped laughing. The situation was very serious, and very real.

"What time is it?" Geneva asked.

"One forty-seven," Millicent replied. Her sister need to take her mind off her problems. Millicent remembered something her father used to do when she had Saturday dentist appointments. To ease the agony, her father would play the wishing game with her. "If you could wish you were anywhere in the world, where would that be?" he'd ask her, or, "If you had a million dollars right now, what would you buy?" It always worked. By the time it was Millicent's turn, she was still thinking about her last wish as she settled in the dentist's chair.

"If you could be in any day in this whole century, which day would you pick?" Millicent asked Geneva.

"Tomorrow!" her sister replied immediately.

"If you had a million dollars right now, what would you buy?"

Soon they heard a horn beep in the parking lot below. Millicent leaped to the window. She recognized her father's car with a yelp of joy. "It's Daddy! He's here!"

He'd made it in record time, he told them, as the three of them drove to the Columbia Hospital for Women, because he knew a lot of side roads. It was snowing harder than ever as they pulled up in front of the hospital. Millicent helped her sister into the wheelchair a nurse rolled to the curb. Her father had called Geneva's doctor and the hospital before they left. And he had pinned a big note on the front door of the apartment, "Gone to the hospital — meet us there," so Mrs. Adams would know where to find them.

Millicent and her father waited in the lobby. He bought her a Coke from the machine and a bag of M&Ms. Soon Mrs. Adams and Rudy rushed through the front doors.

"Are you all right?" she asked Millicent, squeezing her.

"Millicent's had quite a day," Mr. Adams said. "But she did just fine."

"I was so scared," Millicent admitted. "Until Daddy said he was coming. Then I wasn't scared any more. Much."

Minutes later, Lyman burst through the doors. His hair was speckled with snow. He looked as if he had walked all the way from Virginia. But he was grinning happily. "This is a real family affair, isn't it?"

Mr. Adams explained the situation. "Millicent acted with a cool head," he said proudly. "She didn't panic."

"Unlike her brother-in-law," Lyman laughed. "I was definitely not acting with a cool head when she called. I'm going up to be with Geneva now." He gave Millicent a smacking kiss on the cheek.

"Remind me to buy you the biggest box of candy in the world when this is over."

Millicent blushed.

Her mother put her one arm around Millicent and the other around Rudy. "We might as well go home, everybody. It will be a long wait."

# 14

"Blizzard Almost Stops Baby from Being Born" read the headline of Millicent's special edition of the *Wagner Street Chronicle.*

Her headline wasn't quite accurate. The snowstorm, while it left the area blanketed under eleven inches of fluffy new snow, had never reached blizzard proportions, and Geneva's baby would have been born even if Geneva hadn't made it to the hospital in time. That was why babies were sometimes born in taxicabs and at home.

But Millicent thought her headline captured the excitement of the day before. And today! Because today was a no-school day *and* she had a brand-new niece!

Lyman called at four-thirty that morning to blearily announce that Geneva's baby, a little girl, had finally arrived in the world.

"A Valentine's baby," Mrs. Adams said later at breakfast. "Isn't it sweet?"

Millicent had forgotten all about Valentine's day. They were supposed to have a party that day in Mrs. Stann's class and pass out Valentines. Eleven inches of snow was a lot of snow to clear off the roads, so school was cancelled. Millicent hoped her teacher would let them have the party when they went back to school.

After breakfast she gave out the cards she had made for her family and Rudy handed out his. Mrs. Adams stood the Valentines in a row on the mantle. "It looks like we have a lot of people in our family," Rudy had remarked, bundling up to go play in the snow.

"We do," Mr. Adams replied. He was home from work, too, because of the snow. "And now we have one more."

Mrs. Adams was busy making phone calls. Only this time it was not about PTA or playground business. She called *her* mother in Michigan to tell her the news. Grandmother Helena was overjoyed and vowed to fly out for a visit as soon as the weather got better. It had snowed in Michigan, too. Then Millicent talked to her aunt Pat, her mother's sister, who lived in Illinois.

Her mother wanted to call the numerous aunts and uncles and cousins but there were too many and they all lived long distance. That was when Millicent got her brilliant idea. She'd print a special issue of her newspaper, reporting the events of the day before and heralding the arrival of the newest member of their family!

She typed the stories on her father's typewriter, then wrote her famous masthead:

*The Wagner Avenue Chronicle*
The Only Newspaper About Life on
Wagner Avenue, in
Fairfax, Virginia, in
The United States of America, in
The Western Hemisphere, in
The World, in
The Solar System, in
The Milky Way Galaxy, in
The Universe
Millicent T. Adams, Editor-in-Chief

When Mrs. Adams saw the finished newspaper, she was delighted.

"Millicent, this will make a wonderful birth announcement! I'm going to send one to all our friends and neighbors."

Millicent was thrilled. Now everyone would see what an important role *she* played in the whole thing, getting Geneva to the hospital and all.

"But," she said, "the baby doesn't have a name yet."

"She will," her mother, said, smiling. "We can write it on each copy when Lyman and Geneva tell us what it is."

"Daddy isn't going to name the new baby?"

"Oh, no, honey. It's Lyman and Geneva's baby. They'll name their own child."

Millicent wondered if her father was feeling disappointed. He always did the naming in their family. He had named each of them, Geneva and Abigail and Millicent Teresa and Rudy, after a historical figure or some relative who had been dead a long time. When they rented a cottage one time on Deep Creek Lake, Mr. Adams christened it "Bramblewood," which Millicent thought was beautiful. Her father, she admitted to herself, was better at naming cottages than people. She wasn't crazy about her own name, but she was getting used to it.

Then she wondered why her father was so quiet. He was sitting on the sofa, watching Rudy out the window. Rudy was gleefully stomping around in the snow. Why did her father seem so down? Earlier, when Lyman called, her father had been as excited as the rest of the family, but now he was deep in thought again.

Millicent took her newspaper over to him. "Look, Daddy, you were a hero yesterday. I wrote about you coming through the snow to take Geneva to the hospital."

He picked up the single sheet. "Why, so you did. And you didn't even mention the hero has a bald spot."

"Oh, Daddy. Are you ever going to forget that?"

He mussed her hair. "Of course not. What else are fathers for? After your mother gets through running copies for everyone in the civilized world, I'm going to put this with the other newspapers you made. I keep them in a folder."

"You saved my newspapers?" Millicent was surprised. She thought her newspapers went into the trash, along with the other daily papers.

"I save anything my children have done that is precious to me, like your newspapers. And Rudy's drawings. And Abby's anthropology paper, if it ever gets written."

Abby walked into the room. "You may not want to save it," she said gloomily. "It's no good. I have to do it over."

"Writing is hard work," Millicent said. "It took me an hour to write this newspaper."

"I've been working weeks on this dumb paper and it's still awful."

Weeks! Millicent was impressed. The most she had ever worked on a school report was one weekend. Nobody had ever worked so hard on a school paper, she was certain. If anyone deserved to be the favorite child in their family, it ought to be Abby. She earned it.

"Let me see this." Abby took the *Wagner Avenue Chronicle* from her father. "Millicent, this is very good." She looked up, blinking. "Daddy, did I hear you say that you've kept every issue of Millicent's newspaper?" Abby leaned over and impulsively gave Millicent a hug. "You saved my life! Now I know how to fix my paper! I'm going to have my imaginary scientist discover your newspapers!" Abby exclaimed. "It's a terrific device! He'll read them and learn the real truth about the people who live in this house."

"You mean my newspapers are going to be in your college report?" Millicent was flabbergasted. Not only would the *Wagner Avenue Chronicle* be mailed to all their friends and relatives, now it was going to be read by Abby's anthropology professor.

"And what is the truth about the people who live in this house?" Mr. Adams asked Abby.

"Well, the way Millicent writes about us, we sound like a very nice family. Her stories are funny and personal . . . she tells about things no one would ever guess just from looking around at this house." Abby glanced up at the homemade Valentine cards standing on the mantle. "Or maybe they would," she said, smiling sheepishly at her father. "I suppose I've been acting pretty dumb lately, saying our family is too ordinary to write about."

"It all depends on how you look at things," Mr. Adams said wisely.

Mrs. Taylor had said practically the same thing, Millicent remembered. They were talking about being the family favorite. She wondered if her father had been feeling bad because *he* wanted to be the family favorite.

"I've been acting kind of dumb myself lately," Mr. Adams said. "Feeling sorry for myself, because my hair is thinning and a job I wanted went to someone else in the department." He paused.

"Everyone was so busy with their own projects, I thought nobody needed me anymore. Until I got Millicent's call yesterday."

Mrs. Adams had been listening intently. "This is partly my fault. I've been too busy with outside projects. We need to make more time for each other from now on."

Then Millicent said, "I don't mind if your hair falls out, Daddy. We'll always need you."

He drew her to him in a hug. "I know you do. You are all very special and not one bit ordinary. And don't ever forget it."

"And there are no favorites in this family," Millicent declared. "We are democratic. Everybody is liked the same."

The roads were clear enough by lunchtime to venture into the city. It had warmed up, and the snow along the side of roads was already slushy. As Mrs. Adams put it, nothing was going to keep her from visiting her first grandchild.

At the hospital, they went upstairs to Geneva's room. The nursery, where the babies were kept, had special viewing hours but they could visit Geneva any time.

Geneva was sitting up in bed. Her blonde hair flowed over her shoulders in a golden wave. There were bouquets of flowers all over the room, and an enormous bunch of helium balloons from Lyman tied to the end of her bed. Geneva looked very happy to see them. "You're here! I told

Lyman you'd come. He went home to shower and change. He should be back soon. Have you seen the baby yet? Oh, that's right, the nursery isn't open." Geneva looked as though she could barely contain a secret. "Here's a picture of her. It was taken when she was only a few hours old. Isn't she gorgeous?"

They crowded around the snapshot. Millicent was shocked. She was expecting to see a pretty pink-and-white baby, with a bow in her hair. But the infant in the photograph was red and wrinkled-looking, her head shaped like a gumdrop. One eye was pasted shut as if she'd been in a fight. Worse, she didn't even have any hair!

Lyman came in then. He saw Millicent staring at the picture. "I owe you a box of candy — I haven't forgotten. What do you think of my girl? Isn't she beautiful?"

Millicent thought the baby was the ugliest thing she'd ever seen, but she didn't want to hurt her brother-in-law's feelings. She remembered a remark that people often made when they looked at babies. "She looks — just like you!"

For some reason, this made everyone laugh.

Lyman went over to stand beside Geneva's bed. "We have an announcement. In this family, I understand there is a tradition of naming people after special members of the family. I would have liked to name our baby after every one of you, but the baby would have a hard time with six names!"

Laughter erupted once more, only quieter. Mrs. Adams dabbed her eyes with a tissue.

"But Geneva and I have decided that we want to keep up the tradition," Lyman went on. "So we've named our baby Sophia Irene."

"That's my mother's name," Mr. Adams said softly.

Geneva smiled at him. "We thought you'd like that. And now I think the nursery is open. Go see Sophia!"

Since only three people were allowed to view at one time, Lyman escorted Mrs. Adams and Abby down the hall to the nursery. Millicent decided to wait and go with her father and Rudy. She wasn't that anxious to see a homely squint-eyed baby, even with such a pretty name as Sophia Irene.

When Mrs. Adams and Abby returned, they gushed over the baby's beauty. Millicent wondered if they all needed eyeglasses.

It was their turn to visit the nursery. Millicent walked importantly down the hall with her father and Rudy.

The wall of the nursery was mostly glass. There were curtains on either side that could be pulled when viewing hours were over. Inside were rows of plastic cribs. And in each one, covered with a pink or blue blanket, was a new baby. Some of the babies were sleeping. Some were awake and crying, although Millicent couldn't hear them through the thick glass. But their mouths were open and she knew they were crying.

"Which one is Sophia?" she asked, scanning the rows for the ugly, squint-eyed baby in the photograph.

"That one," Mr. Adams said, pointing to a bed in the front row. "That's Sophia Irene."

Rudy hopped up and down impatiently. "Let me see! Let me see!" He was too short to see over the half-wall. Mr. Adams lifted him up.

Millicent steeled herself as she looked. But this baby wasn't ugly at all! She was sleeping, not crying, her pink face turned slightly toward them. She wasn't exactly bald, her light hair was like peach fuzz. Maybe she was more used to being in the world now, Millicent decided.

"Oh, Daddy," she breathed. "Isn't she cute? Look at her tiny little hands! That's my niece!"

"My granddaughter," her father said wonderingly.

Millicent looked up at him. His lips turned up in a soft curve and his eyes were transfixed by the baby in the plastic crib. For the first time in ages, he no longer looked like he was down in the dumps.

"Are you happy, Daddy?" Millicent asked him.

He squeezed her hand. "Yes, I am. You know what? I'm going to donate a ton of pea gravel in Sophia's name. After all, she'll be coming over to our house. She'll play on the new playground."

"I'll show her the tree I saved — we saved," Millicent corrected herself.

"And I'll show her — what'll I show Sophia?" Rudy asked Millicent.

"You can show her your snow saucer."

Mr. Adams laughed. "We can show her everything in the world. It'll all be new to her."

It was like a miracle, Millicent thought. This brand-new person, this baby Sophia Irene with no hair and tiny hands, had made her father happy. One person, she realized, *could* make a difference.

Sophia Irene, unaware of her new status as a miracle, blew a bubble on her lips. The bubble burst, leaving a moist circle on her chin.

Rudy and Millicent giggled. Babies were funny! It was going to be neat to have one in the family.

"This is Sophia's birthday," Millicent said. "It's a special day. Her first day here." February fourteenth, a day to mark in red on the calendar, even though it was already Valentine's Day.

A nurse came to draw the curtains. Visiting time was over. But there would be lots of time to see and play with the baby, Millicent knew.

They walked back down the hall. She held one of her father's hands, Rudy clasped the other.

At the end of the hall a window showed the sun had come out and the snow was glittering.

Millicent said to Rudy, "We haven't ridden your snow saucer down Mrs. Taylor's hill yet."

"Will there still be snow when we get home?" Rudy asked doubtfully.

"The snow will be there," she promised. "We'll have a great time."

And when the snow was gone, they'd still have a great time. They didn't live on Wagner Avenue, home of the world's youngest newspaper mogul and aunt, for nothing.